Samuel French Acting Edition

Clothes Encounters

A Farce in Two Acts

by Roger Karshner

SAMUELFRENCH.COM   SAMUELFRENCH.CO.UK

FOR PRODUCTION ENQUIRIES

UNITED STATES AND CANADA
Info@SamuelFrench.com
1-866-598-8449

UNITED KINGDOM AND EUROPE
Plays@SamuelFrench.co.uk
020-7255-4302

Each title is subject to availability from Samuel French, depending upon country of performance. Please be aware that *CLOTHES ENCOUNTERS* may not be licensed by Samuel French in your territory. Professional and amateur producers should contact the nearest Samuel French office or licensing partner to verify availability.

MUSIC USE NOTE

Licensees are solely responsible for obtaining formal written permission from copyright owners to use copyrighted music in the performance of this play and are strongly cautioned to do so. If no such permission is obtained by the licensee, then the licensee must use only original music that the licensee owns and controls. Licensees are solely responsible and liable for all music clearances and shall indemnify the copyright owners of the play(s) and their licensing agent, Samuel French, against any costs, expenses, losses and liabilities arising from the use of music by licensees. Please contact the appropriate music licensing authority in your territory for the rights to any incidental music.

IMPORTANT BILLING AND CREDIT REQUIREMENTS

If you have obtained performance rights to this title, please refer to your licensing agreement for important billing and credit requirements.

CHARACTERS

ALAN MASTERS, *a real estate broker*

KATHY MASTERS, *his wife, also a real estate broker*

BETTY PARKER

RALPH PARKER, *her husband*

HENIZ, *a handy man*

ACT I

*(At the RISE—early afternoon—we find ourselves in a living room
that constitutes roughly 70% of the SET. A bedroom LEFT ac-
counts for the additional percentage. The living and bedroom
areas are separated by a thin partition and are connected by a
door near the UPSTAGE wall. The living area contains a large
couch DOWN CENTER, angled, fronted by a coffee table. There
is a stand with a lamp and a telephone to the left of the couch, a
couple of easy chairs, and other typical living room stuff like
pictures, a bookcase, TV, etc. There is a desk with a chair facing
the partition LEFT. On this desk is a tomato. But no ordinary
tomato. It is the largest tomato we have ever seen. It is fat, plump,
and gloriously red. Wow! What a tomato! In the wall UP LEFT
is an arched opening leading to a hallway which leads to the
kitchen, laundry room and the rear of the dwelling. To the right
of this archway UP is a closet and to the right of this closet is
another, smaller arched opening leading to the den. An alcove,
accessible by one step, angles off UP RIGHT to the main entrance door. There are double doors in the wall RIGHT which
open to the dining room. In this same wall DOWN RIGHT are a
pair of large French windows above a high sill which are angled
and afford us full view of any action beyond.*

*Now, for the bedroom: against the UPSTAGE wall is a large wooden
wardrobe with double doors. In the wall UP LEFT we find a*

CLOTHES ENCOUNTERS

door leading to the bath/dressing area. A queen-sized bed is set against the wall LEFT. DOWN LEFT, below the bed, is a door leading to a patio. A vanity and a stool DOWN face the audience.

HEINZ ENTERS from the hallway UP LEFT. His is an odd looking little fellow clad baggy coveralls. He has a colorful bandana at his neck. He crosses to the desk and takes up the gigantic tomato, turns it in his hands, studies it admiringly as though it were the Hope diamond. He carefully stuffs the tomato into his coveralls where its presence there creates an enormous protrusion. He waddles from the room humming a nondescript tune. After a few seconds, we hear the sounds of a key rattling away in the front door's lock. It's just a kind of gentle rattle at first followed by louder and louder metallic clattering as the key rattling is escalated due to great frustration. Then we hear bumping and thumping as somebody tries the door. These sounds of heavy pounding, tugging and kicking accelerate to fever pitch accompanied by Alan's disgruntled remarks:)

ALAN. *(Off.)* Now what? These crazy old houses! Firetraps! Junk! Crap!

(The thumping, bumping, and shouting bubble up and boil over. Then, abruptly—silence. Next we see our man in real estate— ALAN MASTERS—approach the French windows. He peers intently into the room then runs his fingers around the window's outer frame, inspecting it gingerly. He pushes inward, and to his surprise and delight the windows give way. He peers into the room tenuously then begins to crawl through the window awkwardly, briefcase in hand. As he crawls through, he catches his foot on the sill and tumbles wildly into the room, his brief case flying,

CLOTHES ENCOUNTERS

its contents scattering like a blizzard of executive snow. Sitting amid his littered papers, he looks about surveying the room with a critical, doleful expression.)

ALAN. *(Cont'd.)* I hate these antiques. All built by a bunch of crazy pioneers who were drunk to the gills on corn liquor. Not worth a damn, any of 'em. Why anyone would want to buy one these firetraps is beyond me. Nothing works, they're drafty, and they all smell like locker rooms. But there's a market for them because people think they're buying into history. Idiots. All they're buying into is eternal upkeep and plumbing so rusty the water looks like root beer. *(He resignedly begins to gather up the papers, still grumbling on.)* People are bent and determined to buy a piece of the past—the frontier. Why on earth would anyone wanna buy a poorly made old house when they can buy a poorly made new one? A least with a rotten new house you get a trash compactor.

(HEINZ ENTERS from the Hallway UP LEFT carrying a watering can with a long spout. He holds up at the sight of ALAN gathering papers, then approaches him quietly from behind and stands observing him with a dopey expression. ALAN, now on his hands and knees, gathering, is oblivious to HEINZ'S hovering presence. HEINZ leans in over ALAN and a few drops of water spill from the can to the top of ALAN'S head. He looks up quickly at the ceiling with an air of suspicion.)

ALAN. *(Cont'd.)* On no! A leak! I might have suspected. The place is falling apart. I hope it doesn't have termites. Or dry rot or shaky timbers or a weak foundation or rusted gutters or poor insulation or bad wiring—or all of the above. You never know with these damned museums. *(He resumes gathering the papers and stuffing them into his briefcase and HEINZ, intrigued, leans in again and this time lets go a torrent of water which fairly soaks the briefcase and many of the papers.)* Aaaaaaah! *(ALAN snaps his head about and reacts with a start at the sight of HEINZ standing above.)* What the—?

HEINZ. Oh! Ferry sorry!

(HEINZ speaks in a language that is Middle-European—maybe. It's a crazy amalgam. Maybe station-house-Dutch, maybe German chocolate cake. Who knows?)

ALAN. And well you should be, for crying out loud! Just look at this mess. Just look at what— *(He gets a load of the enormous bulge in HEINZ'S coveralls and is taken aback. He views the bulge with disbelief and does a long take towards the audience before regaining his composure.)* Just look what you've done to this briefcase—and these papers. *(He grabs up a handful of papers and wrings water from them.)*

HEINZ. They vet?

ALAN. You bet they vet *(Quickly correcting himself.)* —Wet! Of course they're wet, what do you expect? You go and dump Niagara Falls on them and you expect them to stay dry? They're soaked—just look at them. Awwww—No! Nuts! *(He can't believe this is happening to him. HEINZ, however, finds it all greatly amusing.)* So it's funny, is it? Yes, it's funny, all right. About as funny as prostate trouble. There's nothing funny about it. Do you realize you've just ruined multiple copies? *(Waving his hands at HEINZ in a shooing manner.)* Well... just don't stand there with your... *(He is still arrested by the enormity of the bulge.)* with your can hanging out. Go get me a towel, or something. *(HEINZ sets down the can and scurries off towards the hallway.)*

HEINZ. Vun towel, cumink up.

CLOTHES ENCOUNTERS

ALAN. Say, just who are you, anyway?
HEINZ. I'm Heinz, der handyman.

(He EXITS into the hallway like a rat scurrying before a hundred cats.)

ALAN. *(Looking about him with great disgust.)* Yeah, handy all right. About as handy as lint. This house is odd enough without having to contend with a weirdo. *(Very disgruntled, talking to himself as he crawls about picking up the soggy papers which he places in his briefcase.)* God! Look at this mess. A helluva thing to happen to a real estate broker. And Mrs. Parker will be here any minute, too. This old place is going to be hard enough to unload as it is without water stains on the floor, a front door that doesn't work, and some nut running around with a bowling ball in his pants. Sometimes I wish Betty and I had never gotten into real estate. It's not what it cracked up to be. Nights, weekends... And then the thought of Betty showing a house to some pervert... I should've taken over the live bait business from my father like he wanted. So your hands always smell like night crawlers, so what? At least you don't have to sell your soul for a listing. And lately business stinks worse than night crawlers, anyway. If Betty and I don't sell something soon we're in deep trouble. I hope to God I can unload this dump. *(HEINZ ENTERS from the hallway still carrying the watering can and a bath towel identified as—"Hilton". He scurries with it to ALAN who whips it from his grasp roughly and begins wipe his hands.)* So, you're the handyman, huh?
HEINZ. Ya. How you know that?
ALAN. Because you just told me, that's how.
HEINZ. I work for Mr. & Mrs. Merkle for four year now—effer since leaving olt country.
ALAN. Germany. Yugoslavia?

CLOTHES ENCOUNTERS

HEINZ. I don't know.

ALAN. What do you mean, "You don't know?"

HEINZ. All I remember was—it was just old.

ALAN. How can a person not remember what country he's from?

HEINZ. I didn't go outside much.

ALAN. Nonsense.

HEINZ. I stay inside and help Momma with making gruel for ten brothers and sisters. We make gruel in big pot from bread, water, and mashed turnips. Very goot.

ALAN. *(Sickened at the thought. With a screwed up nose.)* Wonderful, I'm sure.

HEINZ. You've tasted turnip gruel?

ALAN. Of course not.

HEINZ. Than how you know it's wonderful?

ALAN. I didn't—don't.

HEINZ. I don't understand.

ALAN. It was merely a statement of irony, that's all.

HEINZ. Huh?

ALAN. Never mind! What do you do for the Merkles?

HEINZ. I do pluming? I do carpenter. I do clean. I do scrub. I do paint. I do wallpaper. I do yard. I do dis, I do dat. I grow garden. Garden is my favorite. Garden is my hobby. Heinz have the biggest cucumber in county.

(This last comment evokes another wide-eyed take towards the audience from ALAN.)

ALAN. *(Wiping his hands, attempting to remain proper.)* Yes...? well... yes, I'm sure you do. Incidentally, I'm Alan Masters—real estate. *(He extends the soiled towel to HEINZ.)* Here. *(As HEINZ steps forward to take the towel he accidentally pokes ALAN between the legs with the watering can's spout. ALAN emits a high-pitched squeal and jumps back gingerly.)* For God's sake, man, watch what you're doing with that thing, will you? *(He takes the attaché to the couch, seats himself, inspects the soaked leather case.)* I think you ruined my Gucci.

HEINZ. *(His hand over the front of his coveralls protectively.)* Ooooh, Gucci. That bad!

ALAN. My briefcase, you numskull—my briefcase!

HEINZ. *(Getting it. Maybe.)* Ahhhhhh.

ALAN. *(Removing soggy papers from the case, shaking them, wringing them out, smoothing them. HEINZ observes this operation with interest.)* Do you have any idea what a case like this costs?

HEINZ. Eight dollars?

(Hovering, encroaching, until he is nearly putting his nose right in the briefcase.)

ALAN. Are you kidding? Say, haven't you got anything better to do?

HEINZ. Nein.

ALAN. How about having a look at the front door?

HEINZ. Why vould I vant to look at front door? Heinz has seen door many times.

ALAN. I mean, fix it. Repair it! There's something wrong with the lock. It's stuck, or something. My key won't work.

HEINZ. Key? How you get key in first place?

ALAN. As if it's any of your business—and it certainly isn't— I have a key because this is a multi-listing.

HEINZ. A valta-pisting?

ALAN. A multi-listing.

HEINZ. A baltic-misting?

ALAN. Mul-ti list-ing!

HEINZ. A ball-tie fist-ing?

ALAN. There's a key out front. In a box.

HEINZ. Vot box?

ALAN. A lock box.

HEINZ. Box locks?

ALAN. A lock box... lock box! With a key for the slot. A lock box! Lock box!

HEINZ. Vot slot? Vot slot dot?

ALAN. The key slot, dot's vot—what!   In the door! *(He mimes putting a key into a lock.)* In the door! Understand? Key! Door! Open! Lock!

HEINZ. Ahhhhhh. Ooooooh. Ah yes! Da lock got slot key from box unlock. Ya?

ALAN. Ya—yes!

HEINZ. We never need locks for house in olt country. People in olt country ferry honest. Never steal nothink. Would never think of coming in house and stealing your cow or goat.

ALAN. Cow or... ? You kept cows and goats in the house?

HEINZ. We had many spare rooms.

ALAN. Hey. You've got to be pulling my leg. *(At this, HEINZ grabs ALAN'S leg and starts jerking it.)* Stop that, dammit! What the hell you think you're doing?

HEINZ. *(HEINZ stops pulling his leg and steps back.)* You say Heinz got to pull leg, so I pull leg.

ALAN. It's a figure of speech, iron head, *(The FRONT DOOR BELL SOUNDS.)*   Ah! That must be Mrs. Parker. *(He rises, places the briefcase on the coffee table and heads towards the alcove leading to the front entrance.)* Coming, coming! *(HEINZ sets down his watering can and briefly studies the briefcase, scratching his head with a muddled expression. Then he takes up the case and its contents and EXITS with it into the hallway leading to the rear of the dwelling. Meanwhile, OFF, Alan is having a hell of a time with the defective entrance door.)* This darn door. Mrs. Parker, is that you?

CLOTHES ENCOUNTERS

BETTY. *(OFF.)* Yes.

ALAN. *(OFF.)* Hold on, the door seems to be stuck. *(Fierce thumping and bumping\ OFF.)* I have an idea. You push while I pull, okay?

BETTY. *(OFF.)* Okay. *(A thunderous amount of racket ensues.)*

ALAN. *(OFF.)* Are you pushing?

BETTY. *(OFF.)* Yes. Are you pulling?

ALAN. *(OFF.)* Yes. But it's not going to work. You'll have to go 'round front to the windows. *(ALAN ENTERS quiclky and begins to cross to the French windows muttering to himself: "This crazy place." "What next?" "A helluva thing to happen," etc. He's across the room when he realizes the door knob has come off in his hand.)* Nuts! The door knob. This stupid barn. *(He rushes back and replaces the knob, and returns in a flash. We see BETTY PARKER appear at the windows.)* I'm really sorry about this.

BETTY. Don't worry about it. *(Extending her hand to him.)* Here, gimme a hand.

(ALAN reaches through the windows and takes her hand and over-zealously yanks BETTY forward causing her to come hurtling through at an unexpectedly rapid rate.)

ALAN. Oops! *(ALAN falls backwards to the floor and BETTY sprawls atop him, her dress up in a revealing manner, just as HEINZ ENTERS from the hallway. He stands riveted, eyes wide, hands clapped to his head at the sight of BETTY lying atop ALAN. He turns and scurries off into the hallway. ALAN rises and assists BETTY to her feet. A real embarrassing interlude for Mr. Real Estate. We note that BETTY is an attractive woman whose low-cut blouse excposs her large endowments. She scrambles to her feet, pulling down her dress over sexy under-garments .)* Gee, I'm sorry. I mean... this is terrible—awful. I'm really sorry, I'm—

CLOTHES ENCOUNTERS

BETTY. Please. No problem, okay? Are you all right?

ALAN. *(Getting to his feet.)* Me? Oh sure—fine. It's just, I mean... it's just kind of embarrassing, you know.

BETTY. A least it was different. And they always say, "you should get close to your broker."

ALAN. I'm sure the door can be easily fixed.

BETTY. I'm sure of it. *(She looks about approvingly.)* My, what an interesting old place.

ALAN. *(A complete switch of attitude.)* Yes. These old homes are wonderful, aren't they? I was just thinking that, just thinking that right before you showed up, about how interesting these old places are. You can't find homes like this today. I mean—with the workmanship, the attention to every detail. The people who put these homes together were serious craftsman. *(Breathing deeply as if savoring a delicious odor.)* These old places just ooze Americana. I can just smell grits baking in the kitchen, and visualize a Southern colonel and his genteel wife sitting on the verandah sipping frosty juleps to the restful sounds of the bayou.

BETTY. In New Jersey?

ALAN. Well... you know. I mean there's like this, this... this overpowering, overpowering—

BETTY. Ambiance?

ALAN. Yes, ambiance, that's the word I was looking for—ambiance. Why, you can just feel the history: Washington, Jefferson—

BETTY. Hamilton—

ALAN. Madison—

BETTY. Jefferson—

ALAN. Andy Griffith.

BETTY. Andy Griffith?

ALAN. Yes, you know. Family, stability, home town values—togetherness! Why anyone would want to buy one of these cheap new homes they build today when he can buy a piece of history like

CLOTHES ENCOUNTERS

this is well beyond me.

BETTY. It does have a certain charm.

ALAN. Some people would trade all this for a stupid trash compactor.

BETTY. Well, I love the grounds—especially the garden. Ralph—Mr. Parker and I—we're a couple of inveterate greenthumbers.

ALAN. No kidding? Really? How coincidental. My wife and I are, too. We find it a very relaxing hobby.

BETTY. How interesting.

ALAN. I had strawberries this year that were as big as apples.

BETTY. You should see my melons.

ALAN. I beg you pardon?

BETTY. I grow the largest watermelons in the county. Ralph and I are very competitive when it comes to our garden. He was furious last year because my melons were bigger than his cucumber.

ALAN. I know the feeling. Kathy can't stand it because my zucchini's so large. But she does wonders with her cantaloupes. She talks to hers. Do you talk to your melons?

BETTY. No, but Ralph carries on long, intellectual conversations with his summer squash. I guess that's because he knows they can't be bored. Ralph has been known to ramble on.

ALAN. Your husband couldn't come along?

BETTY. No. Ralph's out with another salesperson. This way we can look at twice the property, and then compare notes in the evening.

ALAN. Very efficient.

BETTY. I have a feeling he'd love this place, though. Who are the owners?

ALAN. A Mr. & Mrs. Merkle. Very respectable. And they've taken excellent care of the place. New roof, plumbing—repainted just last year. And the baths and kitchen have been completely modernized. It has everything. Even a handyman.

BETTY. Oh?

ALAN. Yes. A strange little fellow. *(Confidential.)* I... I don't think you'd want to keep him, though.

BETTY. Really? Why not?

ALAN. Well, just between you and me—and I hope you don't think I'm stepping out of line—I think he's a bit of a deviate.

BETTY. My! the place does have everything.

(HEINZ ENTERS from the hallway carrying the watering can.)

ALAN. Ah! here it is now. I mean—here he is now. Heinz this is Mrs. Parker—a prospective buyer.

HEINZ. *(Bowing politely.)* Guten tag.

(As he advances BETTY is arrested by the bulge in his coveralls. Her eyes leap from their sockets and she does a long take towards the audience before regaining her composure.)

BETTY. I ah... I... I love your—your garden.

ALAN. Mrs. Parker has the biggest melons in the county. *(HEINZ looks askance at the audience as ALAN crosses briskly, professionally to the coffee table.)* Here, let me show you some details about the property. I have complete information on the place right here in my... *(Baffled by the missing case.)* Right here in my... in my... hum, that's funny.

BETTY. Something wrong?

ALAN. Yes. My briefcase. It was right here on the coffee table just a few minutes ago. Heinz, have you seen my Gucci?

HEINZ. *(With an air of shock.)* Please! Mr. Real Estate.

ALAN. I'm talking about my briefcase—my attaché. The leather thing you were good enough to soak with water like a stupid twit, remember?

HEINZ. Oh, that. Aaaaahhh, ya. *(Pleased at the thought.)* It's spinnink 'round and 'round.

ALAN. Spinning 'round and 'round? What do you mean—spinning? What are you talking about?

HEINZ. Spinnink, you know— *(He mimes spinning, tumbling, while humming some nondescript tune.)* 'Round and 'round. Ofer and ofer. Bump-dee-bump-dee-bump-dee-bump. It's tumblink ofer and ofer and ofer in clothes dryer.

ALAN. Clothes dryer!

HEINZ. *(Proudly.)* Ya.

ALAN. You mean to tell me you put my briefcase in the clothes dryer?

HEINZ. Goot, huh?

ALAN. Goot? Good! Are you kidding, you idiot? Of course it's not good! Who ever heard of putting a leather briefcase in a dryer? *(He makes a bee-line for the hallway.)* Fool! Idiot! Numskull! Gnat brain!

(EXITS.)

HEINZ. *(Making a plea to Betty.)* Heinz only tryink to help Mr. Real Estate

BETTY. Yes, I'm sure you were. *(Moving about, absorbing the surroundings, noting the room with great interest.)* Do you like working here, Heinz?

HEINZ. *(Picking up the watering can.)* Oh, ya. Very goot job. Heinz especially like garden.

BETTY. *(Looking at the ceiling while backing towards HEINZ.)* Well, I'm sure you do good work or the Merkles wouldn't keep you. *(She inadvertently backs her derriere in the watering can's spout.)* Oops! *(She leaps forwards as if hit with an electrical charge, hold-*

ing her rear protectively.) My, you are a little devil, aren't you?

HEINZ. *(Not a clue.)* Thank you.

ALAN. *(ALAN ENTERS from the hallway in a snit, carrying his briefcase which has been reduced to a shattered, lint-encrusted, steaming mass. He is beside himself with frustration.)* Will you look at this? Will you just look at it? Look what you did, you lame brain! *(He stamps his foot petulantly.)* You shrunk my Gucci !

HEINZ. Heinz sorry.

ALAN. You dope! You pin head!

HEINZ. Heinz thought dryer would make it all vell.

ALAN. Vell, hell! You've ruined it! I've got a good notion to have the Merkles take it out of your pay. I'm really terribly sorry about all this, Mrs. Parker. *(Holding up the steaming case with an air of defeat.)* Can you believe this? Heinz, you've got a brain the size of a pencil eraser!

HEINZ. Thank you. *(Smiling, unaware of the fact his response doesn't make bit of sense.)*

ALAN. *(With a clenched fist.)* For two cents I'd—

BETTY. Please—do you think it would be possible to get on with business? The house—remember?

ALAN. Oh yes, yes of course—certainly. The house. Sorry. *(He places the briefcase on the desk and begins to describe the place, moving about the room, indicating with florid hand gestures, speaking with serious pomposity as though he's on the floor of the Senate. HEINZ tags along, aping ALAN, repeating his remarks as though attempting to lend credence. This sincere naiveté is disconcerting to ALAN who is attempting to remain professionally on track.)* Well, first off, all the doors are hand carved and the floors throughout are hand pegged.

HEINZ. Ya—hand-pigged.

ALAN. And your master bedroom has a door that opens to your own commodious patio.

CLOTHES ENCOUNTERS

HEINZ. Your own commode on patio.

ALAN. *(Moving Right, gesturing Right.)* And over here—over here you have a formal dining room. Not just some cramped little hole, which is peeve for any gourmet.

HEINZ. A formal dining room for Steve and Edie Gormet.

ALAN. *(Moving Up, gesturing Up.)* And there's a cozy den with a working fireplace.

HEINZ. Mit verking fireplace.

ALAN. And you have your forced air heating.

HEINZ. Air Force heating.

ALAN. Off the kitchen is a built-in freezer with twenty cubic feet.

HEINZ. Twenty Cuban feet.

ALAN. And the kitchen has been completely remodeled. And there's a laundry room, and a maid's quarters.

HEINZ. *(Correcting.)* No no! Handyman's quarters.

ALAN. *(Unconsciously repeating.)* And a handyman's quarters. *(Spinning about at HEINZ who is practically sitting on his shoulders.)* What the... ? Say, don't you realize I'm trying to conduct business here, man?

HEINZ. But there's no maid. Just handyman.

ALAN. Yes, unfortunately that's the case! Say, haven't you got any work to do?

HEINZ. Verk all caught up.

ALAN. What about getting the front door?

HEINZ. *(HEINZ is nonplused.)* Huh?

ALAN. The front door! The front door! You know—bang bang, kick kick, shove shove? How about getting the door—okay?

HEINZ. Hokey dokey.

(He EXITS dutifully into the alcove leading to the front entrance.)

CLOTHES ENCOUNTERS

ALAN. Idiot. Jerk. Can you believe this crazy character?

BETTY. I think he's kind of cute.

ALAN. Frankly, I fail to see it. *(Heading towards the bedroom.)* Okay, let's start with the master bedroom.

(BETTY follows ALAN into the bedroom.)

BETTY. My, how lovely.

ALAN. Yes?

BETTY. So, the Merkles keep the same bedroom, huh?

ALAN. Apparently.

BETTY. That's nice. That the bloom is still on the rose, I mean.

ALAN. *(Strictly concentrated on real estate.)* Yes. Now, over here is—

BETTY. With us it's the National Geographic.

ALAN. I beg your pardon?

BETTY. The National Geographic has replaced sex.

ALAN. It has?

BETTY. Ralph reads it in bed every night. Has for years. Ever since his Aunt Cora gave him a subscription for Christmas. Last evening when I dozed off he was reading aloud about the Great Barrier Reef. Do you have any idea what it's like being rejected in favor of coral? But even though he's sexually indifferent, he's insanely jealous of me. A very unsettling set of circumstances.

ALAN. Yes. I'm sure. No doubt. Now, here we have—

BETTY. I'm a very passionate woman, Mr. Masters.

(Moving in on ALAN.)

ALAN. *(Backing away shyly, but she pursues him like a tigress.)* Yes, I'm... I'm sure you are.

BETTY. A woman has needs.

CLOTHES ENCOUNTERS

ALAN. Yes.

BETTY. Desires.

ALAN. Of course. Naturally.

BETTY. After night after night of rejection she builds up this overpowering sexual pressure. *(She presses him, and he attempts to avoid her tactfully.)* Do you realize I'm a regular volcano of bubbling, sexual lava?

ALAN. You are?

BETTY. Like Etna.

ALAN. Etna.

BETTY. Vesuvius!

ALAN. Vesuvius.

BETTY. Popocatepetl.

ALAN. Poop-your-cat-a-little?

BETTY. Popocatepetl! It's a volcano—in Mexico. I'm a regular caldron, Mr. Masters, a churning mass of restrained sexual activity that could explode at any minute!

ALAN. Any minute?

BETTY. *(Backing him into a corner.)* Any second!

ALAN. Oh my!

BETTY. People go into marriage like two sticks of dynamite and after a few years they've become nothing but a couple of wet firecrackers. Their wicks are drooping and their power's shot. Why is that, Mr. Masters? Why? *(Running her hands up and down his arms heatedly.)*

ALAN. I... I don't know. This isn't my subject. Ask me about variable mortgages.

BETTY. It's all so sad. It seems like one day you're both in heat, the next you're two married glaciers slowly slipping away to eternity. Can you help me, Mr. Masters? Can you?

ALAN. *(Attempting to gracefully elude her advances.)* Maybe I can get you a favorable loan.

CLOTHES ENCOUNTERS

BETTY. *(Pawing him.)* I mean, help me as a— *(Throwing herself at him, pressing her ample breasts to his chest.)* WOMAN!

ALAN. *(Appalled.)* Mrs. Parker! Please!

BETTY. *(With breathless sensuality.)* Betty!

ALAN. Mrs. Betty! I mean—Parker!

BETTY. What's the matter, don't I attract you?

ALAN. *(Noting her bosom.)* Of course they do. *(Quickly.)* O course you do! But I can't. I mean, I'm just not cut out for this sort of thing. I've never been good at it.

BETTY. I wouldn't mind if your even fair.

ALAN. You'd be disappointed.

BETTY. After all these years with the Geographic, I'll take the chance.

ALAN. It wouldn't work. I know. Until I met Kathy—Mrs. Masters—I was a virgin. I was twenty-nine.

BETTY. Good Lord.

ALAN. For some men it's so easy. It's natural for them to walk up to a woman and say stuff like "What's your sign?" "What time you get off," "How 'bout a cup of coffee?" But I never had the knack. So, I wouldn't want to do anything to jeopardize my marriage. I don't think I could take another twenty-nine years of microwave food. And how you think she'd feel if she found me with another woman? I know I can't stand the thought of her touching another man.

BETTY. You poor thing. *(They react with a start to the sound of violent pounding OFF.)*

BETTY. What's that?

ALAN. Huh?

BETTY. WHAT?

ALAN. I said—HUH?

BETTY. Oh.

ALAN. WHAT?

CLOTHES ENCOUNTERS

BETTY. I SAID—OH.

ALAN. Ah.

BETTY. WHAT?

ALAN. I SAID—AH.

BETTY. HUH?

ALAN. THIS IS RIDICULOUS! I'M GOING TO SEE WHAT'S GOING ON!

BETTY. WHAT?

ALAN. *(Pointing off, screaming at her.)* I'LL BE RIGHT BACK! *(ALAN crosses and ENTERS the living room and BETTY EXITS to the bath/dressing area. ALAN is half way across the living room when HEINZ ENTERS from the alcove carrying a door.)* What the... what the hell is that?

HEINZ. A door.

ALAN. Of course it's a door. I know that. You think I don't know a door when I see one? It was a rhetorical question, you fur brain!

HEINZ. Huh?

ALAN. Rhetorical.

HEINZ. I don't understand.

ALAN. I didn't really mean "what is that?"

HEINZ. But you say,"what is that."

ALAN. I know what I said. Don't tell me what I said! You think I don't know what I said? What I said was, "what is that?"

HEINZ. *(Exasperated.)* It's a door.

ALAN. I know it's a door, dammit! Look—when I said, "what is that?" what I meant was—is, is that I really didn't want to know what it was because when I said, "what is that?" I didn't really say, "what is that?" because "what is that?" didn't require an answer.

HEINZ. Then why ask question?

ALAN. I didn't. I mean... that is to say, "what is that?" really wasn't "what is that?" because I already knew what—that the door

CLOTHES ENCOUNTERS

was a door—that— Aw crap, forget it.

HEINZ. Hokey dokey.

ALAN. What I want to know is, is what in bloody hell you're doing with that door?

HEINZ. You tell me to get door, so I get door.

ALAN. I didn't actually mean get it, you lame brain! I meant "get it."

HEINZ. So?—I get it.

ALAN. I meant fix it!

HEINZ. Then why don't you say, "fix" instead of "get?" First you say, "what is that?" because you don't mean "what is that?" and then you say, "get" when you mean "fix." Vat's matter, you don't know English?

ALAN. Me? Me know English? Now see here you spaced out little— *(He is interrupted by BETTY'S scream OFF. He bolts from the room and HEINZ, shaking his head in bewilderment, EXITS with the door into the alcove. ALAN races across the bedroom and is arrested by BETTY'S emergence from the bath-dressing area. She is toweling her "wet" hair [It would be impractical for the actors to actually be soaked, so they will have to create the effect by toweling, shivering, etc.])* Wha...?what happened?

BETTY. *(Shivering.)* I leaned into the bathtub and turned on the water and it came blasting out of the shower and—God!

ALAN. *(Assuming his mantle of professionalism.)* Let me have a look. *(He goes off stiffly into the bath and BETTY goes to the vanity and begins to check out her hair as HEINZ ENTERS from the alcove with his watering can and goes to a plant Right and attends it. ALAN RE-ENTERS from the bath.)* The faucet's stuck on "shower." I'm terribly sorry about this. I'll pay for the cleaning.

BETTY. It's not your fault. *(Noting herself in the vanity.)* God, look at me. And I'm dripping water all over the carpet. What am I going to do?

CLOTHES ENCOUNTERS

ALAN. I don't know.

BETTY. I'm a mess. I think we should go.

ALAN. Wait a minute. *(He goes quickly to the wardrobe and opens it.)* Look, look here. There's a whole bunch of Mrs. Merkle's stuff in here. Why don't you slip out of your clothes and put on one of her housecoats, or something, and we can look at the rest of the place while your dress is drying.

BETTY. I don't think so.

ALAN. Why not?

BETTY. It just seems a little weird, that's all. I mean—

ALAN. But you can't stay like that.

BETTY. I know, but—

ALAN. You'll freeze to death.

BETTY. I don't think it's a very good idea.

ALAN. Besides, it'd be a shame to leave now without seeing the rest of the place.

BETTY. I don't know. I—

ALAN. I mean, after driving all the way out here, and everything.

BETTY. I'm not sure.

ALAN. Who's going to know?

BETTY. Well... I guess it'd be okay.

ALAN. Of course.

BETTY. *(Running her fingers through her hair, noting the mess in the vanity's mirror.)* Well, I can't go anywhere looking like this, that's for sure. *(Noting two wigs on wig stands on the vanity.)* Say, I wonder if it'd be all right if I wore one of these wigs? My hair looks like over-done spaghetti.

ALAN. Go ahead. The Merkles won't be back till later tonight. *(Moving towards the door.)* While you're changing, I'll go find that crazy handyman and have him fix the shower. *(He EXITS to the living room. BETTY EXITS to the bath/dressing. ALAN spots HEINZ*

CLOTHES ENCOUNTERS

watering the plant and advances upon him. HEINZ, his back to ALAN, is unaware of his presence and when ALAN addresses him at proximity he reacts with a start.) Heinz!

HEINZ. Ja!

(Alarmed, he spins around, turning the water to the front of ALAN'S trousers. ALAN leaps back as though someone has just dumped a load of ice down his pants.)

ALAN. Yeoooooow!

HEINZ. Oh oh!

ALAN. *(Noting a large round wet spot fronting his trousers.)* You idiot! You jerk! You fool! Now look what you've done!

HEINZ. But you give Heinz big scare.

ALAN. *(Wiping at his pants with great frustration.)* Yes, and I'm about to give Heinz a big lip!

HEINZ. Der pants, dey vet?

ALAN. Of course dey vet—wet! What's it look like? Now put down that can before you get into more trouble. *(Wiping at his pants.)* Damn! This is worse than falling out of escrow!

HEINZ. *(Looking upward quickly.)* A crow! Where?

ALAN. No no—escrow! Never mind, never mind! I want you to go take a look at the plumbing.

(During this exchange, BETTY ENTERS from the bath/dressing area wearing sexy under garments, goes to the wardrobe, rifles through it, and withdraws a very sheer, provocative nightie which she slips on. Then she goes to the vanity and removes one of the wigs from its stand and pulls it on, carefully adjusting it to her head.)

HEINZ. Plumbing?

CLOTHES ENCOUNTERS

ALAN. Yes. The shower.

HEINZ. The shower.

ALAN. In Mrs. Merkle's bathroom.

HEINZ. Bathroom?

ALAN. Is there an echo in here, or something?

HEINZ. I don't think so. *(He shouts, hands cupped to his lips.)* Hell-ooooo! Hell-ooooo! Yoo-hoo! Yoo-hoo!

ALAN. *(Stamping his foot.)* Stop that! Now go get a wrench and go take a look at the plumbing. The faucet's stuck on "shower."

HEINZ. Hokey dokey. *(He sets down the can and moves off.)* Vun wrench comink up.

(HEINZ EXITS into the alcove as BETTY ENTERS from the bedroom wearing the sheer nightie which reveals her sexy under-things and a body that would stop traffic. She spins around alluringly, modeling the outfit.)

BETTY. *(Seductively.)* Well?

ALAN. *(His eyes protrude several inches from their sockets.)* Ah... nice—very nice. But wasn't... wasn't there anything else?

BETTY. Oh my! *(Spotting the wet spot fronting his pants.)*

ALAN. What's wrong?

BETTY. I'm sorry.

ALAN. Sorry? About what?

BETTY. I had a cousin with the same problem.

ALAN. Huh?

BETTY. He couldn't hold a thing—

ALAN. What?

BETTY. *(Pointing to the front of ALAN'S trousers.)* —liquids went right through him.

ALAN. Just a minute here, now. You don't think that—

BETTY. It's nothing to be ashamed of—

CLOTHES ENCOUNTERS

ALAN. It isn't like that. I mean—

BETTY. —although you should take precautions.

ALAN. —it's not what you think!

BETTY. They have these diapers on the market now that I understand are very comfortable.

ALAN. You don't understand! It's that hair-brained handyman!

BETTY. Then he should take precautions.

ALAN. No no! He turned his watering can on me!

BETTY. Oooooh, I see—

ALAN. He's either the most inept person in the world or the craftiest, one or the other. *(Pulling his wet trousers away from his body.)*

BETTY. He seems harmless enough to me.

ALAN. I think he's a crafty little weasel. He has a shifty look around his coveralls—eyes!

BETTY. Although he did goose me with his spout.

ALAN. What?

BETTY. With his watering can.

ALAN. Oh. Well, I still think there's more to this little moron than meets the eye.

BETTY. How could there be?

ALAN. I don't trust him. I think it's all an act. Now, how about we get down to it?

BETTY. *(With a seductive purr in her voice.)* Why, Mr. Masters!

ALAN. To the property! To looking at the property. After all, that's what we came out here for, remember? We'll check out the dinning room. *(Moving RIGHT.)* It's huge. You can have the whole family for Thanksgiving dinner.

BETTY. With or without tenderizer?

(As ALAN goes to open the door the knob comes off in his hand.

CLOTHES ENCOUNTERS

Very embarrassing.)

ALAN. *(Fiddling with the knob, attempting to place if back on its shaft.)* Just a... just a screw missing, no doubt.

BETTY. No doubt.

ALAN. *(Securing the knob.)* There. *(They EXIT to the dining room.)*

(As ALAN and BETTY EXIT to the dining room RIGHT, KATHY and RALPH ENTER from the alcove. KATHY is attractive, crisp, business like, and is carrying a briefcase identical to ALAN'S. RALPH is a very stiff and proper.)

KATHY. Strange. I can't imagine what happened to the front door.

RALPH. Termites, you think?

KATHY. Oh no! The place was just inspected. Besides, they couldn't eat a whole door.

RALPH. Don't be so sure. I read in the National Geographic where a termite can eat six times its body weight. It was in the same issue about the pygmies of the Yucatan and how they never get taller because their diet consists primarily of mice.

KATHY. Well, they're aren't any termites around here. Or mice either, for that matter. The property was fumigated just three months ago. *(With an expansive gesture.)* Well, what you think?

RALPH. Hum... interesting.

KATHY. I had a feeling you'd like it.

RALPH. Especially the garden. Mrs. Parker and I love gardening. *(With his hands cupped in front of his chest.)* She has the largest melons in the county, you know.

KATHY. Really? My husband and I love gardening, too.

RALPH. Proper fertilizer's the answer. And watering, of course.

CLOTHES ENCOUNTERS

I've just read an interesting article regarding the irrigation habits of the Peruvian Indians.

KATHY. Really.

RALPH. They've found that a combination of dead earth worms and leeches makes an excellent compost.

KATHY. Fascinating.

RALPH. I've never eaten a worm. Have you?

KATHY. Not recently.

RALPH. I understand they're quite delicious. In many societies worms are considered a delicacy.

KATHY. How facinating.

RALPH. In a current issue of the National Geographic I saw a photo a diminutive aboriginal ingesting a worm four feet in length. Do you ever read the Geographic?

KATHY. Only when I go to the dentist. So, you and Mrs. Parker enjoy gardening.

RALPH. Gardening's a wonderful hobby for a husband and wife. We've become very competitive, however.

KATHY. I know. My husband can't keep his hands off my cantaloupes.

RALPH. I read that in Burma that husbands and wives consider gardening part of their fertility rites.

KATHY. The couple that hoes together, grows together, right? *(She thinks her remark clever, but RALPH remains humorless, stoic.)* Yes... It's too bad Mrs. Parker couldn't be here.

RALPH. She's out shopping with another Realtor. This way we can cover twice the territory. You said your husband's in real estate, too, didn't you?

KATHY. Yes. With a rival firm, actually.

(HEINZ ENTERS from the alcove carrying a large pipe wrench.)

CLOTHES ENCOUNTERS

HEINZ. Oh!

(There is a long period of wide-eyed astonishment as KATHY and RALPH confront the huge bulge fronting HEINZ'S coveralls.)

KATHY. Who—who are you?

HEINZ. My name is Heinz.

KATHY. Oh yes, right—the handyman.

HEINZ. I do carpenter. I do plumbing. I do clean. I do scrub. I do paint. I do wallpaper. I do yard. I do garden. I do—

KATHY. Yes, I'm sure you do. Good to meet you. I'm Kathy Masters, Charles Lucas real estate.

HEINZ. Oooh. Then you got key for slot.

KATHY. Beg pardon?

HEINZ. Key for solt vot unlock *(Pointing toward entrance.)* dot box.

KATHY. Oh... you mean, lock box.

HEINZ. Ya.

BETTY. Heinz, I'm going to show Mr. Parker here through the place, okay?

HEINZ. Parker?

RALPH. *(Stepping forward officially, hand extended.)* Yes, Ralph Parker, glad to know you. *(HEINZ extends the pipe wrench poking RALPH between the legs, causing him to recoil with a high-pitched squeal.)* Hey! Easy with that thing, man!

HEINZ. Heinz fix faucet.

RALPH. What!

HEINZ. *(Breaking Left)* Heinz fix faucet in bathroom. *(As he crosses he mutters to himself, shaking his head incredulously.)* Two Masters, two Parkers, two real estates, two keys dot unlock box vot got slot. *(He EXITS into the bedroom, leaving a befuddled KATHY and RALPH in his wake. Under their dialogue he removes the enor-*

mous tomato from his coveralls and places it carefully on the vanity, removes the bandanna from his neck and drapes it lovingly over the gigantic fruit. He EXITS with the wrench to the bath/dressing area.)

RALPH. My, what a weird little fellow. Perhaps of direct aboriginal descent.

KATHY. I understand he's been with the Merkles for years.

RALPH. *(Noting the water on the floor where ALAN was soaked.)* Hum. I wonder where this water came from?

KATHY. Water?

RALPH. *(Pointing to the spot.)* Yes—right here. Are you quite sure the plumbing is sound?

KATHY. So far as I know.

RALPH. I certainly hope so. These old places can be tricky. And don't forget, that strange little man was carrying a pipe wrench.

KATHY. If I remember correctly, the plumbing was all replaced with brass just two years ago. *(Crosses to the desk.)* Let me check.

RALPH. *(As he speaks KATHY places her attaché on the desk. She notices ALAN'S destroyed briefcase. She holds it up, noting it quizzically, then dumps it into a waste basket near the desk and routs through her own case, finally withdrawing a paper.)* Many civilizations still are without adequate water. In remote regions of the Amazon liquids are extracted from tree bark and the discarded entrails of indigenous beasts. In America we take water for granted. Wasteful. Like over-flushing. Unnecessary, and a carryover from frivolous potty training.

KATHY. Ah! Here it is. *(Pointing to the paper authoritatively.)* Yep, just like I said, all-new copper plumbing just two years ago.

(HEINZ ENTERS from the bath/dressing with the wrench, crosses and EXITS through the patio door.)

RALPH. Good. *(Very business like, rubbing his hands together with anticipation.)* Now how about we take a look through the place?

KATHY. *(Replacing the paper.)* Right. Let's start with the master bedroom.

(She leaves her briefcase on the desk and they cross and ENTER the bedroom.)

RALPH. Lovely. Very spacious.

KATHY. It's a full fifteen by twenty.

RALPH. *(He notices the wet spot where BETTY had dripped.)* Oh oh! Look here— another wet spot. *(Crossing towards the bath/ dressing.)* Something's fishy here. Let me take a look at the plumbing.

(EXITS into the bath/dressing.)

KATHY. God. What else can go wrong? First the front door, then Heinz, and now these inexplicable leaks. I hope the Merkles didn't lie about the plumbing.

(She is shocked by RALPH'S scream Off.)

RALPH. *(Off.)* Yeoooooooooooow! *(He emerges from the bath/ dressing soaked to the skin.)* Ho-ly To-le-do! Look at me!

KATHY. Good Lord!

RALPH. *(Attempting to shake off the water.)* Some flannel-brain has reversed the fixture. The faucet was set on "tub" but when I turned on the water a tidal wave came blasting out of the shower. I'm soaked!

KATHY. How awful! I'm sorry.

RALPH. You're sorry? How do you think I feel? Do you realize I'm a thirty-second degree Mason? I told you the plumbing in this place was suspect. *(Attempting to wipe down his clothes.)* Lord, I'll never get dry!

KATHY. Wait a minute! I have an idea. There's a dryer in the laundry room. Why don't you slip off your wet things and I'll toss 'em in.

RALPH. Are you kidding?

KATHY. They'll dry in a jiffy.

RALPH. Forget it!

KATHY. But look at you.

RALPH. I know, but—

KATHY. You could catch your death.

RALPH. I'm not taking my clothes off!

KATHY. But you can't go anyplace like that.

RALPH. Forget it.

KATHY. But look at you.

RALPH. It's out of the question.

KATHY. But you can't run around like that. And besides, it's crazy to drive all the way out here and not take a look at the place.

RALPH. Well—

KATHY. C'mon.

RALPH. *(Weakening.)* Well... I guess it makes sense.

KATHY. Of course. Who will know? Slip off your clothes while I take a good look at that shower.

(She EXITS to the bath/dressing.)

RALPH. What if the Merkles come back?

KATHY. *(OFF.)* They're not due back till late tonight.

RALPH. Well... okay.

KATHY. *(OFF.)* There's nothing to worry about. Believe me.

RALPH. *(Shouting OFF to KATHY as he removes his shirt and*

trousers.) I wonder why this is so embarrassing? Disrobing, that is. Why, in tribal societies clothing is merely utilitarian, you know. Entire groups spend their lives sans garments and nobody thinks anything of it. To them nudity is nothing. To us—catastrophe. Our mores are stilted and lead to repressed hostilities. No wonder the psychiatrists are having a field day. People are so damned provincial when it comes to body parts. Do you realize that in the upper Amazon there are places never visited by white man? I'd like to go there, but I'd hate to leave my gardening and Betty's beautiful cantaloupes.

(He removes his clothing revealing baggy boxer shorts that strike him at the knees, socks with garters.)

KATHY. *(ADVANCING FROM OFF)(ENTERING.)* Yep, the fixtures are reversed all right.

(Upon seeing RALPH in his ridiculous under things she cannot help but giggle.)

RALPH. What's so darned funny?
KATHY. *(Cutting off her giggling abruptly.)* Nothing, nothing.
RALPH. *(Shivers.)* This place is drafty.
KATHY. It shouldn't be. It's been newly insulated.
RALPH. By the same idiot who did the plumbing, no doubt. *(Alluding to the dress she is carrying.)* What's that?
RALPH. A wet dress I it found hanging over the shower rod. *(She displays BETTY'S dress.)* It must be Mrs. Merkle's. I'll do her a favor and toss it in the dryer along with your things. *(Gathering up RALPH'S shirt and pants. She begins to cross towards the door.)* I'll be right back. *(She crosses and ENTERS the living room and EXITS into the hallway. RALPH looks about then goes to the wardrobe, opens it and routs through its contents roughly like a bargain hunter*

CLOTHES ENCOUNTERS

at a sale. He withdraws a pair of pants and attempts to pull them on. An impossible task because they are ridiculously small. He struggles and hauls and tugs, and pulls. To no avail.) Good Lord! This fellow Merkle must be a jockey. *(He tosses the pants back into the wardrobe and routs about in it, finally pulling out a sheer, boa-trimmed dressing gown. He studies it for a few seconds, then gives a broad shrug of resignation and quickly pulls it on. He then goes to the vanity mirror and checks himself out. Noting himself with disgust, he pulls a toupee from his head and wrings it out.)* God, look at me. A few minutes ago I walked in here a gentleman and now look—a bald-headed drag queen. *(He shakes out the toupee and then places it on the bed, spreading it out carefully. KATHY ENTERS from the hallway and crosses to the bedroom and reacts with humorous disbelief at RALPH.)* Don't you dare laugh.

KATHY. Well... it's different.

RALPH. It's all I could find, okay? I'm doing my best. At least it'll keep me from freezing to death in this wind tunnel. All right, let's get on with it. The sooner I see this place and get out the better.

KATHY. Let me show you the kitchen.

RALPH. All right. But for God's sake—don't turn on any water.

(KATHY and RALPH cross and ENTER the hallway as BETTY and ALAN ENTER from the dining room.)

BETTY. Very nice.

ALAN. Perfect for large parties.

BETTY. And formal. Ralph would like that, he's very proper.

ALAN. *(Glancing into the alcove.)* Oh, no! That idiotic gnome still hasn't put the front door back on.

BETTY. *(Crossing.)* I'll go see how my dress is doing.

CLOTHES ENCOUNTERS

(She goes into the bedroom and ENTERS the bath/dressing area.)

ALAN. I had a feeling things were going to be strange today when I woke up and all the digital clocks were blinking. Then I spilled my oatmeal in the toaster and it burned up and set off the smoke alarms. Days are like soda crackers—so many are gonna be broken no matter what the hell you do.

(He reacts to BETTY'S ANGUISHED CRY and blots into the bedroom as BETTY emerges from the bath/dressing.)

BETTY. It's gone!
ALAN. What's gone?
BETTY. My dress!
ALAN. Gone?
BETTY. Yes.
ALAN. How could it be gone?
BETTY. I don't know how, but it is!

(ALAN dashes into the bath dressing and pops immediately out again wide-eyed.)

ALAN. It's gone!
BETTY. I told you.
ALAN. But... I mean, where could it go? It doesn't have legs. Unless you're in it, that is.
BETTY. Now what am I going to do?
ALAN. *(Panicking, racing about hysterically, in a panic, looking into and under everything.)* The main thing is, is not to panic, to keep cool, to think clearly, to remain calm, to keep a clear head and not lose our composure, to stay relaxed, to not to become emotional or over-wrought. It's got be around here someplace. It just has to be.

CLOTHES ENCOUNTERS

Ask yourself, where would you go if you were a dress? *(He bolts into the living room in a panic and begins to search as BETTY scours the bedroom.)*

BETTY. Now let me see, where would I go if I were a dress?

(ALAN drops to his knees in front of the couch, looking under. KATHY and RALPH ENTER from the dining room, cross and EXIT to the den UP just as HEINZ ENTERS from the hallway carrying the dress, shirt, and pants. He is noting them quizzically, scratching his head. He goes to the closet, deposits the stuff inside and then crosses and EXITS into the alcove just as KATHY and RALPH come from the den, cross, and ENTER the hallway. Alan continues his search for a few beats, then:)

RALPH. *(Off. In a shrill, high-pitched, panicked voice.)* Where the hell are my pants?
ALAN. *(Looking up with a start in the direction of the bedroom.)* Oh no! Now her panties are missing, too? *(Beat.)* Heinz? Nooooooo, he can't be that crafty.

(He resumes searching on his hands and knees in front of the couch, peering under. BETTY ENTERS the bath/dressing as KATHY ENTERS from the hallway, looks about, drops to her knees and crawls behind the couch. RALPH crawls around the end of the couch as KATHY crawls from around the same end. They suddenly come facr to face.)

ALAN & KATHY. Yeeaaaaaaahhhhhhhhhh!

(They spring to their feet wearing looks of stark incredulity.)

CLOTHES ENCOUNTERS

ALAN. Kathy!

KATHY. Alan!

ALAN & KATHY. What are you doing here?

ALAN. I... I—I'm waiting for a client! What about you?

KATHY. What about me what? Oh! I'm waiting for one, too—a client, that is! But, but what were you doing on the floor?

ALAN. I... I was looking for... for a cufflink! Yes—a cufflink!

KATHY. But, you're not wearing French cuffs.

ALAN. *(Checks his buttoned-cuff shirt sleeves and responds with an odd giggle of embarrassment.)* Ah! Yes! Right. Then that must be the reason I can't find it! What about you?

KATHY. What about me what?

ALAN. Why were you on the floor?

KATHY. Me? Oh, I... I ah—I was checking for termites!

ALAN. Termites?

KATHY. Yes. *(Pointing towards the alcove.)* Like the ones that ate the front door! Like the Yucatan pygmy termites who can eat six times their body weight in National Geographic!

ALAN. What the hell are you talking about? The handyman did it.

KATHY. He ate the front door!

ALAN. *(Anguished.)* No no! He removed it because I said "get it" when I only meant "get it" and he thought I said "get it" so he got it. Get it?

KATHY. Alan, are you okay?

ALAN. Of course I'm okay. Certainly. Why wouldn't I be okay?

KATHY. *(Noticing the large water stain fronting his pants.)* Alan, I never knew you had that problem.

ALAN. What problem?

KATHY. *(Pointing at his trousers.)* Weak kidneys.

ALAN. The handyman did this.

KATHY. No!

CLOTHES ENCOUNTERS

ALAN. He got excited and let it go all over the front of me.

KATHY. What a disgusting habit.

ALAN. He runs around sticking it into everything.

KATHY. No!

ALAN. Have you met him?

KATHY. Heinz? Yes. He came in awhile ago with this big thing in his hand.

ALAN. *(Incensed.)* What? Why, that—that perverted dwarf!

KATHY. It looked like some kind of wrench, or something.

ALAN. *(Relaxing somewhat.)* Oh. Well, I'd still keep an firm eye on him. He's an odd little duck.

KATHY. He seemed harmless enough to me.

ALAN. Don't kid yourself. He's a crafty little vermin. A wolf in sheep's coveralls. By the way, when is you client getting here?

KATHY. Client?

RALPH. Yes, your client.

KATHY. Oh yes—client! Any minute, any minute. What about yours?

ALAN. What about mine what?

KATHY. Your client. When's he getting here?

ALAN. Oh—any minute! And that reminds me—I wanna check the place out first, get oriented, get the lay of the land, you know.

KATHY. Yes. Right. Good idea. Me too. Check it out—get the lay of the land.

ALAN. *(Silly laugh.)* I wanna be sure everything's okay, in working order, copacetic, you know.

(Stupid chuckle.)

ALAN. *(Easing towards the bedroom door.)* Right. Copacetic. *(Dumb laugh.)* I'll ah—I'll catch you later, okay?

KATHY. Sure, fine. *(Waving her fingers cutely.)* Toodle-loo.

CLOTHES ENCOUNTERS

ALAN. Toodle-loo.

(He ducks into the bedroom, slams the door and leans against it breathlessly and KATHY slumps to the arm of the couch with a sigh of great relief but hastily stands as RALPH ENTERS from the hallway. BETTY ENTERS from the bath/dressing. The following lines are delivered in a panicked, rapid-fire, nearly overlapping manner:)

KATHY. You won't believe this!
ALAN. You'll never believe this.
RALPH. Believe what?
BETTY. What?
ALAN. My wife!
KATHY. My husband!
RALPH. What about him?
BETTY. What about her?
ALAN. She's here!
KATHY. He's here!
RALPH. No!
BETTY. No!
ALAN. Yes!
KATHY. Yes!
RALPH. No!
BETTY. No!
ALAN. With you like that, and my wife a jealous nut, it'll be the end of my marriage. She'll never understand.
BETTY. Who would? You think my husband will?
ALAN. We've got to get out of here.
BETTY. I'm not leaving without my dress!
KATHY. We have to get out of here.
RALPH. Not till I find my pants!

CLOTHES ENCOUNTERS

KATHY. *(Pointing towards the den.)* Okay. You look in the den. I'll check the bedroom.

(RALPH EXITS to the den and KATHY goes to the bedroom door and attempts to open it but it is blocked by ALAN'S leaning against it. ALAN and BETTY freeze. KATHY tries the door again, putting her shoulder to into it, but it doesn't give. ALAN points frantically to the wardrobe and BETTY scurries to it and EN-TERS. ALAN leaves the door and makes a mad dash for the wardrobe and ENTERS also, closing its door behind them. KATHY lunges at the door which implodes with a gush sending her sprawling. HEINZ ENTERS from the patio and, for the moment, does not see KATHY due to her sprawled position behind the bed. He notes the toupee atop the bed, places it in his cover-alls. He crosses to the night stand, pulls the bandanna from the tomato and gathers it up. As he turns he spies KATHY and re-acts with a start.)

HEINZ. Oh!

KATHY. *(She is equally shocked at the sight of the weird little man with the gigantic tomato.)* Oh, Heinz! *(She rises, attempting to regain her composure as quickly as possible.)* I didn't see you come in.

HEINZ. I come through patio.

KATHY. Oh, I see. *(She notices the enormous tomato in HEINZ'S hand and reacts with wide-eyed disbelief.)* Oh, Heinz— my! What's that in you hand? It that yours?

HEINZ. *(Proudly.)* Ya.

KATHY. My heavens! I've never seen one like it!

HEINZ. Ya. Heinz very proud.

KATHY. I think you should be, it's beautiful. And so plump and big.

CLOTHES ENCOUNTERS

(The wardrobe shakes slightly but neither HEINZ nor KATHY notice due to their intense involvement with the tomato.)

HEINZ. When Heinz was little boy he neffer dream of having one dis big.

KATHY. I'd love for my husband to have one that size.

HEINZ. I had the biggest in olt country.

KATHY. I'll bet you did. Would you mind... I mean... would it be all right if I felt it?

(Again, a noticeable shaking of the wardrobe. Also a high-pitched whine.)

HEINZ. Ya. But be careful not to squeeze too hard.

KATHY. My, it certainly is something!

HEINZ. It's a whopper all right.

KATHY. And sooooo smooth!

HEINZ. Ya.

(The wardrobe shakes. Another whine.)

KATHY. How'd it ever get so big?

HEINZ. I spend lots of time with it.

KATHY. It feels good.

HEINZ. Heinz have trouble keepink hands off it himself.

(There is a muffled shriek from the wardrobe which causes KATHY to look up sharply.)

KATHY. What was that?

HEINZ. Vot vas vot?

KATHY. Dot—that! That noise?

HEINZ. Heinz don't hear nothink.

KATHY. I could have sworn.... Oh, well. *(Returning the tomato to HEINZ.)* You'd better put that away before something happens to it. And thank you.

HEINZ. Yer velcome.

(He EXITS through the patio door and KATHY scans the room for the pants. Satisfied that they are not available she leaves room, slamming the door behind her, crosses the living room and EN-TERS the den. After a few seconds one of the wardrobe doors opens ever so slowly and ALAN peers out and looks about cautiously before climbing out. BETTY follows. ALAN, ashen, stands motionless for a few seconds then clenches his fists and lets out a primitive scream.)

ALAN. Aaaggghhhhhh! *(He slumps to the bed, face in hands, a depressed mess. BETTY places a consoling arm about his shoulder.)* My dear wife. Can you believe it?

BETTY. No. Some women have all the luck.

END OF ACT ONE

ACT II

(Immediately following. ALAN and BETTY are holding the same positions—ALAN seated on the bed dejectedly, KATHY standing over him.)

ALAN. I had a feeling this would happen one day. That in one of these strange houses with some pervert she'd cave in to underlying feminine urges. Women are like trains. They go chugging steadily along on the same old track for years, always on time, dependable, and then—just when you're convinced they're reliable—a little emotional cinder gets on the rails and off they go in all directions like a mass of hurtling steel. But I never dreamed it would be with such a disgusting person as this. You'd think she'd have at least chosen a normal person instead of some over-endowed elf. Maybe it's my fault for talking her into going into real estate, maybe it's the pressure of escrow, maybe it's due to my lack of sexual imagination. I've never been very adventuresome, not one for bedroom gymnastics or any of that. It's got to do with my childhood, I think. With an over-protective mother who always threw her purse in front of my face when ever there were animals mating.

BETTY. These things happen.

ALAN. Not to real estate brokers.

BETTY. There has to be an explanation.

ALAN. Yes, you're right. And the explanation is that degenerate shrimp.

BETTY. Not so little, apparently.

ALAN. Mrs. Parker! Please!

BETTY. Do you think, maybe—under the circumstances—we could make it Alan and Betty?

ALAN. The sawed-off viper forced himself on her, took unfair advantage. I should have never doubted Kathy for a second. She's not the type. You can bet I'm giving a full account of this to the Merkles. That over-sexed little weirdo will be on a boat back to someplace-or-other within a week.

BETTY. *(Dreamily.)* It seems such a loss.

ALAN. *(Getting defiantly to his feet.)* Just wait till I get my hands on that diminutive rat!

BETTY. First, we have to get our hands on my dress.

(KATHY ENTERS the living room from the den still searching for the missing pants. She falls to her knees and once again peers under the couch.)

ALAN. Dress? Oh, yes, yes, right—the dress! Well, let's get looking. And please—keep yourself out of sight. *(BETTY resumes her search and ALAN leaves the room and ENTERS the living room and spots KATHY on all fours near the couch. BETTY goes into the bath/dressing area.)* Kathy! *(Surprised, she looks up.)* What are you doing down there?

KATHYDown where?

ALAN. On the floor, where do you think I mean?

BETTY. Oh, I'm... I'm—I'm checking for rats!

ALAN. Rats?

KATHY. Yes. Rats—sofa rats.

ALAN. Sofa rats?

KATHY. Yes. Very rare and insidious creatures.

CLOTHES ENCOUNTERS

ALAN. I've never heard of such a thing.

KATHY. They get into sofas and breed. Have like these huge families. They take over. Run rampant. They can eat up a couch in twenty minutes. *(Rising, dusting her hands with an air of brisk, professional finality.)* Well, no sofa rats.

ALAN. Kathy, how could you?

KATHY. How could I what?

ALAN. C'mon, you know what I'm talking about.

KATHY. You mean... look for sofa rats?

ALAN. Don't try to be cagey.

KATHY. Cagey?

ALAN. I'm talking about you and that man.

KATHY. Man? What man?

ALAN. Don't try to play dumb with me. You know who I'm talking about.

KATHY. But, Alan, it's not what you think. It was all so innocent, believe me. He turned on the shower and—

ALAN. I just overheard you with him in the bedroom.

KATHY. The bedroom?

ALAN. Yes, the bedroom, just a few moments ago.

KATHY. Oooooh—you mean Heinz.

ALAN. Of course I mean Heinz. Who do you think I'm talking about?

KATHY. But it was nothing.

ALAN. Nothing?

KATHY. Yes.

ALAN. You call that—nothing!

KATHY. Yes.

ALAN. Of course, I'm not blaming you you understand. It's that stunted pervert! He forced it on you.

KATHY. Forced what on me?

CLOTHES ENCOUNTERS

ALAN. C'mon, you were looking at it, even feeling it. Don't try to deny it.

KATHY. Oh, that.

ALAN. That's not just a "that." That's much more than a "that."

KATHY. But I wanted to see it.

ALAN. Kathy!

KATHY. I just couldn't keep my hands off it.

ALAN. *(Pounding the couch with great frustration.)* NO, NO, NO!

KATHY. Alan, what's gotten into you?

ALAN. *(Nearly in tears, shouting to the ceiling.)* She just couldn't keep her hands off it! My own wife! The woman I split commissions with.

KATHY. If you ever saw it you'd want to touch it, too.

ALAN. *(Suddenly indignant.)* Now hold on just a minute here. What do you take me for?

KATHY. It's so beautiful.

ALAN. *(Wringing his hands with frustration.)* This just can't be happening.

KATHY. It was so nice and plump and—

ALAN. Please, spare me! No details! Besides, I understand perfectly—you were compromised. *(His frustration lapses into anger.)* Just wait till I get my hands on that can of sauerkraut! *(Heading in the direction of the den.)* He's got to be around here somewhere.

(KATHY, remembering that RALPH is in the den, reacts quickly by throwing herself in ALAN'S path.)

KATHY. No no! Not in there!

ALAN. So now you're hiding him, huh?

KATHY. Yes. I mean—no! Of course not.

ALAN. *(Attempting to pass.)* Get out of my way, Kathy!

CLOTHES ENCOUNTERS

KATHY. No! He's not in there. He ran out. *(Pointing towards to entrance hall.)* He went that way.

ALAN. Oh, he did, did he? *(Striding boldly towards the alcove.)* Just wait till I get hold of that pint-sized sex fiend.

(He EXITS. KATHY goes to the den and opens the door.)

KATHY. All clear. Come on out. Quick!

RALPH. *(Sticking out his head cautiously.)* Where'd he go?

KATHY. He went to kill Heinz.

RALPH. *(ENTERING from the den.)* Well, let's get looking while we have a chance. I want to get out of this madhouse.

(KATHY and RALPH EXIT into the hallway. HEINZ ENTERS the bedroom from the patio. He's carrying two giant tomatoes and the pipe wrench. He crosses to the wardrobe, places the wrench on the floor, and then places the tomatoes out of harm's way atop the wardrobe. He retrieves the wrench and EXITS to the bath/dressing area as ALAN ENTERS from the patio.)

BETTY. *(Off.)* YeeeooooooooowwwwwW!

(HEINZ springs from the bath/dressing area as though shot from a cannon.)

HEINZ. *(Cowering.)* Heinz mean nothink! Didn't see lady bending over.

ALAN. *(Suddenly ENTERING from the patio, advancing on HEINZ menacingly.)* Oh, you didn't did you? Why, you little ape! Attacking another poor, innocent woman with that... that thing! What kind of man are you anyway?

HEINZ. *(Circling away from the closing ALAN.)* A handyman.

CLOTHES ENCOUNTERS

ALAN. No you're not! You're a degenerate in hot coveralls!

(The men circle slowly, ALAN relentlessly pursuing HEINZ who is backing away, attempting to maintain a safe distance. HEINZ backs up and over the bed and ALAN, in his pursuit, crosses the bed also. It is a tense, cat and mouse situation. BETTY ENTERS from the bath/dressing area to witness the men circling the room.)

BETTY. What are you going to do?

ALAN. I'm going to put out this little titmouse's lights, that's what.

HEINZ. Mr. Real Estate, please!

BETTY. Don't do anything rash.

ALAN. *(His hands extended in a strangling manner.)* This isn't rash, this is premeditated. This is something I'm going to enjoy. If I had video camera I'd tape it so I could watch it every day in prison!

HEINZ. Help!

BETTY. Stop!

HEINZ. Heinz do nothink!

ALAN. Oh yeah? Do you call forcing that thing on my wife, nothing?

(They circle. Up and over and around.)

HEINZ. Force what?

ALAN. Don't try to play dumb with me, you mini-greaseball. I heard you in here. I heard you showing it to her?

HEINZ. Oh! Oh dat.

ALAN. Yes, dat—that!

HEINZ. But it's Heinz's pride and joy.

ALAN. What? Good God! Don't you have any shame, man?

CLOTHES ENCOUNTERS

(KATHY pops in from the patio. BETTY freezes.)

KATHY. Alan! What in heaven's name are you doing?

ALAN. I'm putting out the fire in this pervert's pants!

KATHY. No!

ALAN. Don't try to stop me—

KATHY. *(Noticing BETTY.)* Alan!

ALAN. Don't bother me while I'm committing murder.

KATHY. Alan! *(Pointing.)* Who is that woman?

ALAN. Woman? What *(Grasping situation.)* Wo-wo-wo-woooooo-wooooooo... *(He emits a dopey laugh as all action freezes. ALAN looks furtively between BETTY and KATHY as HEINZ looks on from atop the bed.)* Oh! you, you mean— *(Pointing towards BETTY.)* that woman? Why ah... why that's ah, that's—

BETTY. *(Saving the moment.)* I'm, Mrs. Merkle.

ALAN. You are?

BETTY. Yes.

ALAN. Oh yes!—yes you are! She is! Yes. Mrs. Merkle, I mean.

HEINZ. *(Indicating with his pipe wrench.)* Dot not Mrs. Merkle.

ALAN. Shut up you slimy SOB!

KATHY. I... I thought you were gone for the day.

BETTY. I came back early.

ALAN. Yes—unexpectedly.

BETTY. Very.

HEINZ. *(Sensing a great opportunity to escape.)* Bye bye.

(He springs from the bed and ALAN pounces on him bringing him to the floor where the men roll about wildly in each other's clutches.)

KATHY. Alan, for heaven's sake, stop it!

HEINZ. Listen to your vife!

ALAN. You creepy little weasel!
HEINZ. Me not veasel! HELP!
KATHY. Stop it! Make them stop it, Mrs. Merkle!
BETTY. Let go of that veasel—weasel!

(ALAN wrests the pipe wrench from HEINZ who leaps to his feet and blots off into the living room. ALAN, wrench in hand, gives chase with KATHY racing after. BETTY stands rooted, flabbergasted.)

KATHY. *(Running behind ALAN.)* Alan, stop! *(The trio races into the living room, around the couch, serpentine through other furniture with HEINZ screaming for mercy, ALAN shouting threats, and KATHY bellowing for ALAN to cease the madness. They tear off into the alcove. Much screaming and shouting OFF. BETTY EXITS to the bath/dressing area. RALPH ENTERS from the hallway cautiously, crosses and goes into the bedroom. He goes to the bed and discovers his toupee is missing. He reacts with a start.)* My hair! It's gone!

(He bolts about, muttering to himself, looking for his toupee. He looks quickly through the wardrobe then goes to the vanity and begins to rifle it. ALAN ENTERS breathlessly through the patio door and comes to an abrupt halt at the sight of RALPH in his outfit. RALPH is holding a purse he has just removed from the vanity. There is an embarrassed silence.)

ALAN. Who... who are you?
RALPH. *(A trapped closet drag queen.)* Me? Why... why... I'm... I'm—I'm Mr. Merkle! *(Without a word, with a look of blank bewilderment, ALAN turns and blots through the patio door, leaving RALPH with a vacant expression. RALPH returns the purse to the*

CLOTHES ENCOUNTERS

*vanity's drawer, goes to the DOWNSTAGE side of the bed, drops to
his knees and begins to search under. Now we see Heinz's face come
up at the windows. He peers into the room carefully then crawls
through the window, tiptoes across the room, ENTERS the bedroom,
and goes directly to the wardrobe. He reaches up in order to re-
trieve his tomatoes but is thwarted in his attempt by Ralph's voice
emanating from the far side of the bed.)* Where the hell are my pants
and toupee?

*(HEINZ, panicked, pops into the wardrobe just as RALPH rises.
KATHY ENTERS from the hallway, crosses and goes into the
bedroom, locking the door behind her.)*

KATHY. We have to clear out of here—fast!

RALPH. I can't leave like this.

KATHY. Nobody will notice you in your car.

RALPH. And what do you propose I tell my wife when I get
home? That I've just been to Denmark? I'm not leaving here without my pants! And now my toupee's missing, too.

KATHY. But Mrs. Merkle is home!

RALPH. No!

KATHY. She was right here in this very room just a few moments ago.

RALPH. Oh no! And I think I just met your husband—sort of.

KATHY. Alan?

RALPH. A real square dresser with a pained look like he's chok-
ing on a hair ball?

KATHY. That's Alan. How'd you explain yourself?

RALPH. I told him I was Mr. Merkle.

KATHY. What?

RALPH. I was on the spot! It's not like I'm in this situation
every day, you know. In some strange house, out of my pants, out of

my hair. Just look at me. Just look—*(He spots the giant tomatoes atop the wardrobe.)* Wow! Just look at those! *(He crosses and takes the tomatoes from the top of the wardrobe.)* My, what magnificent specimens. Wonderful. Just feel the weight of these. *(He hands the tomatoes to KATHY who hefts them in her hands. ALAN ENTERS from the hallway carrying the pipe wrench and as he makes a cross he is arrested by the sound of KATHY'S voice from the bedroom. He goes to the bedroom door and listens.)*

KATHY. Aren't they beautiful!

RALPH. The nicest I've ever seen? *(ALAN attempts to peek through the keyhole but no luck. He presses his ear to the door.)* They're perfect.

KATHY. Yes. You don't see them this size very often, do you?

(ALAN'S head comes up short.)

RALPH. Not often enough. Here, let me hold them.

(ALAN is beside himself. He shakes his fist. He tries the door but the knob comes off in his hand. He is totally frustrated.)

KATHY. What do you think?

RALPH. They're so firm, so smooth—and such a beautiful color.

KATHY. Be careful. Don't bruise them.

(ALAN is coming apart.)

ALAN. The fiend!

RALPH. How I'd like to sink my teeth into these.

(ALAN prances, and whines with anger.)

CLOTHES ENCOUNTERS

ALAN. I'll kill him! I'll kill him! So help me God, I kill the perverted pigmy!

RALPH. I'll bet they'd be delicious with mayonnaise.

ALAN. *(At his boiling point, brandishing the pipe wrench wildly.)* Why that kinky little creep! *(He can restrain himself no longer and begins to pound the door violently.)* Open up! Open up in there!

(KATHY and RALPH freeze.)

KATHY. You think he heard us?

(KATHY looks about, her mind turning at high RPM, then motions towards the wardrobe. ALAN continues to pound and shout things like "Come on, I know you're in there," "Open up, you deviate," etc. RALPH jumps into the wardrobe with the tomatoes and KATHY quickly pulls a colorful housecoat from it and slips it on. She then seats herself at the vanity and dons the other wig and pair of sun glasses she finds on the table.)

ALAN. All right! Okay! That's it! No more messing around! You asked for it! *(He steps back, lowers his shoulder and rushes the door just as KATHY rises and opens is. ALAN comes hurtling through, tumbling like a load of wet wash into a great heap near the bed where he reacts with astonishment at the presence of a well-disguised KATHY standing above him.)* Oh! I'm, I'm terribly sorry, Mr. Merkle—

KATHY. *(Her dialect defies description.)* Me not, Mr. Merkle.

ALAN. *(Rising, dusting himself off.)* —I didn't mean to.... You're not?

KATHY. Nien. I'm Frieda, Heinz's vife.

CLOTHES ENCOUNTERS

ALAN. Heinz's vife?—wife? Oh my. You poor woman.

KATHY. Vot you vant mit Heinz?

ALAN. *(Displaying the wrench.)* I have a nice pipe wrench for him.

KATHY. I haffen't seen him. I think Heinz at market buyink knockvurst.

ALAN. I could have sworn I heard him in here just a moment ago with my wife.

(Looking about suspiciously.)

KATHY. Mit yer vife?

ALAN. Yes.

KATHY. Heinz could neffer be in bedroom mit other man's vife.

ALAN. You poor, innocent thing.

KATHY. Heinz is a ferry loyal husband.

ALAN. Ignorance is bliss, I guess. *(He reacts to a sneeze from the wardrobe.)* What was that?

KATHY. *(Blatantly naive.)* Vot vas vot?

ALAN. That noise?

KATHY. Vot noise? *(Another sneeze.)*

ALAN. There it was again.

KATHY. Dare vas vot again?

ALAN. The noise. You didn't hear it?

KATHY. I don't hear nothink. *(Another sneeze.)*

ALAN. *(Whirling about, pointing in the general direction of the wardrobe.)* There is was again! It came from that spot over there.

KATHY. Vot spot?

ALAN. *(Pointing, attempting to make her understand in her own "tongue," what ever it is.)* That. I mean—dot. *(Pointing.)* Dot!

KATHY. Dot vot?

ALAN. Dot's the spot!

CLOTHES ENCOUNTERS

KATHY. Huh uh. *(Pointing off in the opposite direction.)* Dot is spot?

ALAN. *(Getting crazy.)* No no! Not dot spot! *(Pointing in the direction of the wardrobe.)* Dot's the spot!

KATHY. Nein. *(Pointing at wardrobe.)* Not dot spot. *(Pointing in the opposite direction.)* Dot's der spot!

ALAN. No no! Dot's not der spot.

KATHY. Ya, dot's da spot.

ALAN. Na. I mean—no!

KATHY. Da spot I got is spot vot got noise. Da spot I got make noise a lot, dot's vot. But dot spot you got not spot vot got noise because dot spot you got—

ALAN. *(Going nuts with frustration, jumping up and down with his fists clenched. He's a child having a tantrum.)* Stop it! Stop it! I can't stand it! *(Another sneeze.)* Ah ha! The wardrobe!

KATHY. Vordrobe?

ALAN. Is there an echo in here?

HEINZ. *(From wardrobe.)* Hell-ooooooo! Yoo-hoo!

ALAN. Ah ha! There's someone in that wardrobe!

KATHY. Oooh. Must be dog.

(She barks like a dog.)

ALAN. Dog? Are you trying to tell me that the Merkles keep a dog in the wardrobe?

KATHY. No no. Vordrobe made of dogwood.

ALAN. *(Closing on the wardrobe.)* That's the silliest thing I've ever heard of.

KATHY. *(Attempting to block his advance.)* No no, vardrobe bite!

ALAN. *(Sweeping her aside.)* Nonsense, woman.

CLOTHES ENCOUNTERS

(He goes to the wardrobe, opens the right hand door, peers in at the density of clothing, and then crawls in. As he enters the right hand door, HEINZ EXITS the left and runs out through the patio. Then RALPH EXITS, places the tomatoes on the vanity, and tears out after him. ALAN can be heard thumping and bumping, making muffled threats inside the wardrobe. HEINZ runs back into the room and crosses to the vanity.)

KATHY. What the.... ? What are you doing back here?
HEINZ. Heinz forget tomatoes.

(He snatches up the tomatoes and makes a dash for the bedroom door. Much to his dismay the door is stuck and he wrestles with it desperately.)

KATHY. Hurry!
ALAN *(From wardrobe. His leg appears as he backs from the cabinet.)* I can't understand it. I could have sworn I heard something in there.

(HEINZ is frozen with fear.)

KATHY. Quick—the bed!

(HEINZ shoots across to the bed, throws back the covers and jumps in, covering himself quickly just as ALAN backs fully from the wardrobe. HEINZ is an obvious shivering mass beneath the covers.)

ALAN. I could have sworn I.... *(He holds up as he spots the quivering lump under the covers.)* AH HA! So, there you are! *(He descends on the bed with the pipe wrench.)*

CLOTHES ENCOUNTERS

KATHY. Vot you goink to do?
ALAN. I'm doing this for your own good, Mrs. Heinz.

(He takes a pillow from the bed and begins to flail the quivering form of HEINZ who screams wildly under the fusillade. Then, suddenly, HEINZ throws back the covers and sits upright, a look of stark agony playing across his features.)

HEINZ. YOU SQUASHED MY PRIDE AND JOY!

(He fairly catapults from the bed and races out the patio door. ALAN races madly after.)

ALAN. Come back here you ingrate!

(He EXITS. The sound of screams and shouts OFF. Then the men burst from the alcove, cross the living room, race into the bedroom ,and once again out through the patio door. Sound of screams and shouts OFF. HEINZ bolts in from the hallway and hides in the closet UP as Alan appears. He looks about for a few seconds, befuddled by HEINZ' escape, then blasts off into the alcove. BETTY ENTERS from the bath/dressing area and encounters KATHY.)

BETTY. Oh! Who are you?
KATHY. Me Frieda, Heinz vife!
BETTY. I didn't know Heinz had a vife—wife!
KATHY. I'm just comink over from olt country.
BETTY. I see. Well, I'm Mrs. Merkle. So, you're Heinz's wife, huh? My, what a fortunate woman.
KATHY. Ya.

CLOTHES ENCOUNTERS

BETTY. You must go to sleep every night with a smile on your face.

KATHY. Usually mit cold cream.

BETTY. I meant—contentment. By the way—just between us girls—is it a large as they say it is?

KATHY. Begging pardon?

BETTY. You know... *(She holds her fingers in a manner indicating roundness.)* Heinz's pride and joy.

KATHY. Ooooh, that. Ya, even bigger.

BETTY. Oh my! How exciting. Just a quirk of nature, I guess.

KATHY. Oh no! Because of fertilizer.

BETTY. Fertilizer?

KATHY. Ya. He sprinkle lots of fertilizer on it effer spring.

BETTY. Really? I'll have to get Ralph to try that.

KATHY. Ralph?

BETTY. Mr. Merkle.

KATHY. Ya, goot idea. Then maybe he vin prize like Heinz.

BETTY. Prize? You mean they have contests?

KATHY. Ya, vunce a year. *(Backing away.)* Vell, Frieda, must go now. Must get holt of Heinz.

BETTY. Yes, I can certainly understand why you would want to.

KATHY. *(Backing from bedroom door.)* Vel, auf wiedersehen.

BETTY. Auf weidersehen.

(KATHY leaves the bedroom, peels off the wig and glasses and dumps them into the waste basket near the desk and EXITS to the hallway as ALAN ENTERS the bedroom from the patio.)

ALAN. The little creep gave me the slip. Now, we have to clear out of here fast. Mr. Merkle is in the house, too.

BETTY. God! The place is crawling with Merkles.

CLOTHES ENCOUNTERS

ALAN. He's a very strange fellow, incidentally. Weird.

BETTY. I can't leave looking like this. My dress just has to be around here someplace.

ALAN. I've looked high and low. You'll have to leave like that.

BETTY. And what do you propose I tell my husband?

ALAN. And what do you propose I tell my wife if she finds you're not Mrs. Merkle? In that outfit, she'll think you're a prostitute.

BETTY. A prostitute!

ALAN. Please! Keep your voice down.

BETTY. This was your idea, Mr. wise-guy-real-estate-broker—remember?

ALAN. Okay okay, all right! Calm down, please! I'll have another look around. But please keep out of sight, for Pete's sake.

(ALAN EXITS to the patio, and BETTY returns to the bath/dressing as KATHY ENTERS the living room from the hallway and looks about the room searchingly. She goes to the closet, flings open it's door, and leaps back in fright as HEINZ steps out with an air of jaunty confidence. He is wearing RALPH'S shirt and trousers which are greatly oversize, sunglasses, has a large-brimmed hat pulled very low over his face, and is carrying a walking stick. He's standing on his tiptoes in order to gain stature. He's a very comical, aberrant sight indeed.)

KATHY. Oh! Who... who are you!?

HEINZ. *(Attempting to disguise his thick accent.)* I... me? I... Mr. Merkle!

KATHY. *(Still in semi-shock, hand to her bosom.)* Oh! Mr. Merkle. Whew! *(She extends he hand professionally.)* I'm Kathy Masters, real estate. *(HEINZ, groans, pulls his hat even lower in an attempt to keep from exposing his face fully.)* You gave me quite a fright for a minute there. I'm here waiting for a client. I was just checking out the closet space. *(A clumsy laugh.)* You have a lovely home. And a beautiful garden.

HEINZ. Ya—yes! Lovely.

KATHY. I just love the feeling of this old place. *(She turns, offering a sweeping gesture at the living room, and HEINZ accidentally gooses her with the walking stick. She squeals an seemingly becomes airborne for a few seconds. ALAN ENTERS from the alcove.)* Oh, Alan! I'd like for you to meet Mr. Merkle.

HEINZ. *(A low groan.)* Oooooooh.

ALAN. That isn't, Mr. Merkle.

KATHY. Alan! How rude. He just came out of the closet.

ALAN. Oh! Oh well. In that case, he's Mr. Merkle. *(Extending his had to HEINZ.)* We met awhile ago in the bedroom, remember? Alan Masters, real estate.

(HEINZ emits a muffled grunt as he shakes ALAN'S hand.)

KATHY. I was just telling Mr. Merkle what a lovely place he has here.

ALAN. *(Eyeing "Mr. Merkle" suspiciously.)* Yes, lovely.

KATHY. I think my client will love it. He should be here any minute now. What about your client, Alan?

ALAN. *(Circling, attempting to get a better view of "Mr. Merkle" who is doing his best to avoid his leer.)* Client? Oh yes— client. She... she'll be here any time.

(Titters stupidly.)

KATHY. *(Easing herself toward the hallway.)* I think I'll ah... take a look at the basement. Nice meeting you, Mr. Merkle.

CLOTHES ENCOUNTERS

(HEINZ nods, taking great care to hide his countenance under the hat's brim. KATHY EXITS into the hallway. There is awkward silence between ALAN and "Mr. Merkle." Then ALAN begins to pace while speaking pompously in oratorical tones.)

ALAN. Mr. Merkle, I don't know exactly how to put this. I mean, it's not easy for a man in my position—an Elk, a member in good standing of the local Rotarians—but I feel it's my duty to inform you regarding your handyman, Heinz. Now I realize he's been with you for many years, and I'm sure he's a good worker, and a trusted employee, but there are certain aspects of his personality which, quite frankly, I consider odious. In all honesty—and I'll attempt to put this as tactfully as possible—I think the man may be slightly unbalanced in the sex department. I mean, after all, parading around with that... that thing, and exposing it to everybody. The man has no shame. I know this a serious accusation, Mr. Merkle, but twice today he's forced himself on my wife, breaking down her resistance. To put it bluntly, I'm afraid your man Heinz is an insidious pervert. I feel sorry for his nice little wife.

HEINZ. Vife? Er—wife!

ALAN. Yes. We had a most revealing encounter in your bedroom.

HEINZ. *(Hands to his cheeks.)* Encounter. Ooooooooow!

ALAN. She's a charming little thing.

HEINZ. Encounter. Ooooooooow!

ALAN. I'm sorry I had to break this to you, sir, but I felt you should know. After all, the little deviate—fellow—is in your employ. Now, if you'll excuse me, I have some things to check out before my client gets here.

(He EXITS into the alcove.)

CLOTHES ENCOUNTERS

HEINZ. *(He goes quickly to the phone and dials.)* Hello, Helga. I vant you to know I hear about your encounter and I'm fileink for divorce. *(He slams the receiver with a note of finality.)* All these years Heinz been livink with a tramp.

(He reacts to the voices of KATHY and RALPH approaching OFF. He races to the closet and hides inside as KATHY peers into the room from the hallway followed by RALPH'S head craning around the jamb. They give the impression of two wide-eyed geese peering around a corner. They ENTER cautiously, looking from side to side.)

RALPH. So, old man Merkle is in the house too, huh?

KATHY. Yes. And a weird acting little fellow too, I might add.

RALPH. Well, Merkles or no Merkles, all I care about is finding my clothes and clearing out of here.

(They react to ALAN's voice Off.)

ALAN. *(Approaching, Off, Calling.)* Kathy?

KATHY. Oh no! *(She opens the closet, and shoves RALPH inside just as ALAN ENTERS from the alcove. She greets Alan with a contrived innocence, and a dumb laugh.)* Oh, Alan.

ALAN. That's snake's hiding around here someplace, I can feel him. Where's, Mr. Merkle?

KATHY. I thought he was with you.

ALAN. I gave him an earful about Heinz.

KATHY. Alan, it was no big thing.

ALAN. Kathy, Please! Look, I'm willing to forget the whole thing. I'm sure you were caught in a compromising situation.

KATHY. What are you talking about?

CLOTHES ENCOUNTERS

ALAN. Men like him often have a hypnotic effect on women. They— *(There is a crash from within the closet.)* Wha—what was that?

KATHY. *(Covering.)* What was what?

ALAN. That noise.

KATHY. What noise? I didn't hear any noise.

(There is another crash from the closet. KATHY shows no reaction to the commotion.)

ALAN. There! There it was again.

KATHY. *(Cool.)* There was what again?

ALAN. You mean to tell me you didn't hear that?

KATHY. I didn't hear anything. You sure you're feeling all right?

ALAN. I think it came from the closet.

(He moves toward to closet.)

KATHY. *(Blocking his path.)* No!

RALPH. No, what?

KATHY. No, it didn't come from the closet. It... it came from... from—the attic! Yes, the attic! *(Pointing ceilingward frantically.)* It's bats!

ALAN. Bats?

KATHY. Yes, the Merkles don't have termites, but they have a bat-infested attic. They're up there crashing into everything. You know, blind as bats?

(Her story is blown by another crash from the closet.)

ALAN. Nonsense. *(Stepping toward the closet.)* Something's going on in that closet.

CLOTHES ENCOUNTERS

KATHY. *(Doing her best to restrain him.)* Alan, no!

(ALAN pushes past her and as he is about to open the closet door when it pops open and Ralph steps out wearing an air of supreme confidence.)

ALAN. Mr. Merkle!
KATHY. Mr. Merkle?
ALAN. But you seem taller.
RALPH. Taller than what?
ALAN. And... what happened to your pants?
RALPH. That's a good question.

(A loud crash from the closet freezes them all.)

ALAN. What was that!?
KATHY. *(With a shrug.)* Bats?

ALAN. Bats hell! *(He steps to the closet and flings open the door and HEINZ steps out, hat low, walking stick in hand, wearing sunglasses.)* Mr. Merkle?

RALPH & HEINZ. *(Simultaneously.)* Yes?
ALAN. All right now, what's going on around here? You both can't be Mr. Merkle.
RALPH & HEINZ. Yes.
ALAN. *(Beside himself.)* Dammit! What do you take me for, anyhow?
RALPH. We met when you came running into the bedroom with that thing in your hand. Remember?
KATHY. What!
ALAN. The pipe wrench! Okay then, if you're Mr. Merkle—

CLOTHES ENCOUNTERS

(Turning to HEINZ.) then who the devil are you?

    HEINZ. *(With his head low.)* Mr. Merkle.

    ALAN. *(Stamping his foot childishly.)* Stop that! You both can't be Mr. Merkle. Now which one of you is Mr. Merkle?

    RALPH & HEINZ. I am.

    RALPH. *(Dawning on him that HEINZ is wearing his clothing.)* Oh yeah? *(Pointing feverishly at HEINZ.)* In that case, what are you doing in MY PANTS!?

(HEINZ jumps back, inadvertently prodding ALAN between the legs with his walking stick, causing him to rise on his toes and squeal shrilly.)

    HEINZ. *(Having a complete lapse of identity.)* Oh! Ferry sorry, Mr. Real Estate!

    ALAN. What? *(He whisks the hat from HEINZ'S head exposing his nemesis. HEINZ shrinks several sizes.)* Why, why, why you, you—

(He advances upon HEINZ threateningly.)

    KATHY. Alan, control yourself!

    HEINZ. *(Cowering, backing away from the advancing ALAN.)* Poor Heinz, he do nothink!

    ALAN. I'll show you nothing, you little ferret!

    KATHY. Stop it!

    HEINZ. Please!

(He blots towards the alcove and ALAN springs after him.)

    RALPH. *(Lurching off after them.)* Stop him! He's in my pants!

    ALAN. *(In hot pursuit, racing into the alcove after HEINZ.)*

CLOTHES ENCOUNTERS

He's in everybody's pants!

(The men EXIT into the alcove, leaving KATHY stupefied. Shouting and screaming OFF. Then the men ENTER through the patio door in the following order: HEINZ, ALAN, then RALPH, shouting— "No! Stop!" "Stop him!" "Help!" "Sex fiend!" "I do nothink!" "My Shirt!" "Please!" "Degenerate!" "No!" "Stop those pants!" "You squashed my tomatoes!" "Deviate!" "Help!" etc. The men race over the bed. HEINZ darts into one side of the wardrobe, followed by his pursuers. They spurt from the other side, EXIT the bedroom, and bolt across the living room into the hallway. Whooping and shouting OFF. They charge in from the alcove like bulls in heat, HEINZ still in front, RALPH now second, ALAN last. They circle the couch, stream into the bedroom, and out the patio door. Shouting and whooping and screaming OFF. KATHY stands riveted, her hands to her head. The men explode from the hallway in reverse order—ALAN first, RALPH second, HEINZ last. They reach the center of the living room before they discover the absurdity of their order. They come to a screeching halt, all do a "what the hell" take and then bolt off into the hallway in logical order—HEINZ in lead, ALAN second, RALPH in the rear. Whooping and shouting fades in the distance OFF. KATHY finally comes unglued and races wildly into the hallway. Then BETTY ENTERS from the bath/dressing area and crosses the bedroom and ENTERS the living room where she resumes searching for her dress. She runs about in a state of heightened desperation overturning pillows, looking under this and that. She opens the closet and routs through it roughly and reflects the joy of discovery.)

BETTY. Ah ha! Finally. My dress.

CLOTHES ENCOUNTERS

(She takes her dress from the closet, drapes it over the couch and slips out of the see-through nightie revealing sexy under garments—garter belt, etc. She reacts to the sound of approaching screaming, whooping and hollering OFF, snatches up her dress, grabs the nightie, and pops into the closet simultaneous with HEINZ'S hasty ENTRANCE from the alcove. He looks about nervously, locked momentarily in fear, not knowing which way to turn. Then he speeds to the closet, pops into it, closing the door behind him. ALAN rushes in from the alcove as RALPH rushes in from the hallway. Then men streak in opposite directions, RALPH EXITING the alcove, ALAN EXITING the hallway. KATHY ENTERS from the Hallway, crosses and goes into the living room just as ALAN races in breathlessly from the alcove.)

ALAN. *(Looking about.)* Damn! He slipped through my fingers again.

KATHY. That poor man.

ALAN. Poor? I'll show him poor. Just let me get my hands around his filthy neck!

KATHY. Heavens! Get hold of yourself.

(ALAN strides to the closet boldly, and swings open the door exposing BETTY standing there in panties, bra, garter belt, etc. She is, however, exposed to the audience only, not BETTY whose attention is directed DOWNSTAGE. The blood drains from ALAN'S face, his eyes widen to panicked orbs. He slams the door quickly.)

ALAN. Well, nothing in there! *(He emits a strange, weak cackle.)* Maybe Mr. Merkle caught him.

KATHY. If he did, he could have his hands full.

CLOTHES ENCOUNTERS

ALAN. What!

KATHY. He may put up a fight. *(Her attention is arrested by naughty giggling from the closet.)* What was that?

ALAN. *(He is a portrait of angelic innocence.)* What was what?

KATHY. That sound?

ALAN. What sound? I didn't hear anything, dear.

(Again, naughty giggling from the closet.)

KATHY. There. There is was again!

ALAN. There was what again?

KATHY. That sound.

ALAN. What sound?

KATHY. It sounded like it came from the closet.

ALAN. *(An alter boy.)* Closet?

(More giggling from the closet.)

KATHY. *(Advancing towards the closet.)* Yes—the closet.

ALAN. *(Putting himself between KATHY and the closet.)* Stop!

KATHY. Alan!

ALAN. You don't want to open that door!

KATHY. *(Attempting to pass him.)* Will you please move!

ALAN. You'll be sorry! I'll be sorry! Everyone will be sorry!

KATHY. *(Attempting to push past him.)* Do you mind?

ALAN. It could be embarrassing. What if it's Mr. Merkle changing into one of his outfits?

KATHY. It sounded like a woman to me.

ALAN. Well?

KATHY. Alan, will you please get out of my way?

(Another spasm of high-pitched, sexy giggling.)

CLOTHES ENCOUNTERS

ALAN. It could be the dreaded Closet Mice!

KATHY. What?

ALAN. Closet Mice. A very large, kinky breed of rodent. You open that door and God only knows what they'll be up to in there. I hate to think about it!

KATHY. *(Pushing past him.)* Don't be silly.

ALAN. *(Sensing the game is up.)* No! Kathy, I can explain. It's all so innocent. She went to look at the shower and—

(KATHY opens the door, and BETTY steps out immediately, calmly, closing the door behind her. She is wearing her dress, no wig, her hair is down normally.)

BETTY. *(She is cool and casual, showing no trace of panic or anxiety. As if she steps from a closet to greet strangers every day.)* Hello.

KATHY. *(Her voice cracking.)* H-hello.

BETTY. I'm Betty Parker.

ALAN. *(Still in a state of nervous shock.)* Parker?

BETTY. *(Glaring at him.)* Your client—remember?

ALAN. Oh, yes—certainly! Yes! Of course! My client! *(Smiling, fidgeting awkwardly, laughing stupidly.)* Of course! Mrs. Parker.

BETTY. Betty Parker

KATHY. No relation to Ralph Parker by any chance?

BETTY. Why, yes, he's my husband. Do you know him?

KATHY. Do I ever.

BETTY. Beg pardon?

KATHY. It just so happens that's who I'm waiting for. He's my client.

BETTY. Ralph? Really? No! My, what a small world.

ALAN. *(Chuckling weirdly.)* Yes, I was just thinking that. About the world, I mean, how small it is, you know. Little. *(Ridiculous titter.)* Oh, by the way, this is my wife, Kathy.

BETTY. Well, good to know you. *(Extending her hand to ALAN.)* And good knowing you, too, Mr. Masters.

ALAN. *(Feeble attempt at humor.)* It's good to be known.

(A dumb laugh which is not shared by the women.)

BETTY. I didn't find anyone around when I arrived so I decided to take a look for around for myself. I was just checking out the closet to see if it was cedar lined. No problem, I hope?

ALAN. Problem? Oh, no! No problem. None at all. Don't give it a thought.

KATHY. A nice property, don't you think?

BETTY. Oh yes, very.

ALAN. How about I show you the rest. Will you excuse us dear, while I show Mrs. Parker—

BETTY. Betty.

ALAN. Betty. While I show Betty through the rest of the place?

KATHY. Sure.

ALAN. *(Moving RIGHT.)* We'll check out the dinning room. It's huge. You can have the whole family for Thanksgiving dinner.

BETTY. With or without tenderizer?

ALAN. *(Forced laugh.)* That's very funny. Nothing I like better than a client with a sense of humor, Mrs. Parker.

BETTY. Betty.

ALAN. Betty.

(They EXIT to the dinning room leaving KATHY looking after them with a blank expression. Behind her, HEINZ opens the closet door carefully and peers out. He steals from the closet, once again wearing his coveralls, and tiptoes off into the alcove.

CLOTHES ENCOUNTERS

RALPH ENTERS from the hallway in a frustrated, exhausted state.)

RALPH. He got away. And in my shirt and pants. Just the thought of that strange little person in my clothes makes me sick to my stomach. I don't believe this day. When I got up this morning things were boringly normal. I like things boringly normal. This way you don't built up distracting expectations. But after being in this fun house for ten minutes my whole life is a jumble of uncertainty. Do you realize how disruptive this is for a man who just finished reading a nice, tranquilizing article about the rings of Saturn? What else can go wrong?

KATHY. Plenty. Your wife is here.

RALPH. What? You have to be kidding!

KATHY. *(Pointing to the dinning room.)* She's here. Right now. In this house. She's in the dining room tenderizing her relatives.

RALPH. No!

KATHY. She's my husband's client. Can you believe it? Of all the people in the world. She showed up just a few moments ago.

RALPH. Oh my God! *(Looking down at his outfit.)* And look at me. What if she sees me like this? What in the world will I tell her?

KATHY. That you're trying out for a part in Gypsy?

RALPH. Very funny. This is it! My marriage is over! All those nice cozy evenings with her and the National Geographic, the two of us doing home shopping on E-bay—the gardening. She'll take her big, beautiful melons someplace else. This is it. This is the end, this is the—

(He is interrupted by the approaching voices of ALAN and BETTY approaching from the dinning room. A look of horror grips his face.)

CLOTHES ENCOUNTERS

KATHY. Quick—the closet!

(She opens the closet door, and shoves RALPH in just as ALAN and BETTY emerge from the dinning room.)

BETTY. Very nice. I like it.

ALAN. You don't find many homes with formal dining rooms these days. Do you, Kathy?

KATHY. Do I what?

ALAN. Find houses with formal dining rooms? And I was telling Betty how everything has been updated: The plumbing, kitchen, baths, roofing, insulation—even the wiring. *(Moving towards the closet.)* Here, let me show you. The new control panel is in the back of the closet.

KATHY. *(Leaping in front of him ,blocking his progress.)* No!

ALAN. Kathy! What the—

KATHY. The... the panel! It's not in the closet!

ALAN. Yes it is. Now let me pass.

KATHY. They moved it. It's... it's in the garage!

ALAN. *(Attempting to pass her.)* No it isn't. It's in the back of the closet.

(Pushing he aside.)

KATHY. You don't want to go in there!

ALAN. Why not?

KATHY. Mr. Merkle, remember?

ALAN. Oh!

BETTY. Mr. Merkle, the owner? I'd love to meet him.

KATHY. No you wouldn't!

BETTY. I wouldn't?

KATHY. No!

CLOTHES ENCOUNTERS

ALAN. Because he's... he's—eccentric! Odd.

KATHY. Odd?

ALAN. Different.

KATHY. He likes clothes.

BETTY. So what? So do I.

ALAN. Women's.

BETTY. Oooooh, I see. One of those, huh? Oh well, I'm a big girl. Besides, it's his business. *(She pushes past them and opens the door, and RALPH steps out boldly wearing his shirt and pants. On his head, ludicrously replacing his toupee, is the wig BETTY had deposited in the closet when she made her change.)* RALPH!

RALPH. *(Feigning surprise beautifully.)* Betty!

BETTY. What in the world—?

RALPH. I had an appointment to look at the place but when I arrived no one was around so I decided to check it out for myself. What about you, dear? What are you doing here?

BETTY. Same as you. I'm here to look at the property.

ALAN. Really? Well I'll be. Isn't this a coincidence?

KATHY. Yes, isn't it. *(Stepping forward professionally, extending her hand.)* I'm Kathy Masters, your salesperson. This is my husband, Alan.

ALAN. I'm showing the house to Mrs. Parker.

BETTY. Betty.

ALAN. Betty.

RALPH. My, this is a coincidence.

(He laughs awkwardly triggering a round of polite, awkward laughter.)

BETTY. Ralph, what in the world have you got on your head?

RALPH. Head? Why it's my— *(He pulls the wig from his pate, and studies it with a shocked expression before recovering immedi-*

CLOTHES ENCOUNTERS

ately with aplomb.) It's my new toupee. *(He slams the wig back to his head where it rests comically askew like a stuffed muskrat.)* I decided that it was time for a change. Time to... to get hep.

BETTY. I think the term is "hip," dear.

RALPH. Hip, yes, right—hip. Time to get hip, to liven up my image, to get with it, with what's happening, and all that. I read in the National Geographic where man is constantly seeking new levels of expression. The Bantus, for instance, change headdress each year before eating raw reptiles. And the tribes of the upper Congo express their creativity by utilizing the juices they extract from the livers of young wildebeest for the rites of Spring—

KATHY. Ralph.

RALPH. Yes, dear?

KATHY. Shut up.

RALPH. *(Quickly changes gears.)* Yes. Well.... *(Looking about approvingly, rubbing his hands.)* Well ah... what do you think of the place, Bette?

BETTY. I love it. You?

RALPH. With this garden your melons will be bigger than ever. *(Turning to KATHY.)* We'll take it!

BETTY. We will?

ALAN. Terrific!

KATHY. Yes. Wonderful.

BETTY. Yes. But on one condition, Ralph.

RALPH. What's that?

BETTY. The handyman stays.

(There is polite, strained laugher all around.)

CURTAIN

CLOTHES ENCOUNTERS

PROP LIST

Two large tomatoes, or facsimiles
Two identical briefcases
One tiny, shriveled briefcase
Professional looking documents
Watering can
Bath towel inscribed "HILTON"
Door knob
One door
Two womens' wigs
Sexy nightie
Sheer dressing gown
Pipe wrench
Man's toupee
Two pair of sunglasses
Walking stick
Wide-brimmed hat